DISCOVERY AT COYOTE POINT

Avon Flare Books by
Ann Gabhart

ONLY IN SUNSHINE

ANN GABHART lives on a small farm in Kentucky with her husband and three children. She enjoys bird-watching and walking in the woods and fields with her two dogs. When she's not writing, she's working in her vegetable garden or reading. She's had two historical romances published as well as several novels for teenagers.

DISCOVERY AT COYOTE POINT

ANN GABHART

DISCOVERY AT COYOTE POINT is an original publication of Avon Books. This work has never before appeared in book form.

AVON BOOKS
A division of
The Hearst Corporation
105 Madison Avenue
New York, New York 10016

Published by arrangement with the author
Library of Congress Catalog Card Number: 88-91369
ISBN: 0-380-75497-5
RL: 4.4

First Avon Camelot Printing: May 1989

Printed in the U.S.A.

OPM 10 9 8 7 6 5 4 3 2 1

In memory of my father,
J. H. Houchin,
who passed on to me his love of places like Coyote Point

DISCOVERY AT COYOTE POINT

CHAPTER 1

I stood at the window and watched the taillights of Mom's car disappear around a curve. Then I watched awhile longer hoping Mom would change her mind and come back for me.

While I stared at the empty road, her words echoed in my mind. "A year's not really very long, Ance. You'll see. I'll be home before Christmas comes again, and this will give you a chance to get to know your father's people better."

I turned away from the window slowly, still not quite able to believe Mom had actually gone without me. Grandmother Sanford was waiting for me with an uncertain smile.

"Maybe you could get the box down from upstairs, Ance, and help me take down the tree," she said. "We have to do it today. You know it's bad luck to leave a Christmas tree up till after New Year's."

"Luck ain't so easy to bribe," Grandfather Sanford said from his chair by the stove. Even as he spoke, he scooted the rocking chair around, opened the stove door, and poked at the glowing red log inside. Satisfied that the fire was burning as hot as it should, he slammed the door shut.

"Don't pay him no mind," Grandmother said. "He's cross as an old bear in the wintertime."

"I wish I was an old bear asleep in some cave over at Coyote Point," Grandfather said.

Grandmother ignored him as she began picking the crinkled icicles off the cedar tree one by one. "The box for the Christmas ornaments is upstairs in the room across from yours, Ance."

I looked from my grandmother to my grandfather. I didn't know them very well. In the five years since my father had died when I was seven, I'd only seen them a few times. As my throat tightened, I looked back out the window, but the road was just as empty as it had been a few minutes ago. I was here, like it or not, for the next year.

When I came back downstairs with the box, Grandmother was still carefully lifting the icicles off the skinny cedar tree. Dried out by the heat of the stove, the tree was a pretty sorry-looking affair, but as Mom had said last night when we arrived, no doubt Grandmother had put it up especially for me.

I started to pull one of the glass balls off the tree, but Grandmother stopped me. "The icicles first, Ance. Then the ornaments."

I stuck the glass ball back on its branch and

began grabbing at the icicles. The cedar made my hands itch.

"You're just like Russell," Grandmother said. "He loved getting the tree in and setting it up, but I always had to make him help take it down." She took the icicles I'd gathered and put them with hers. Then she tried to smooth out the tangles I'd gotten in mine before she put them in the little box that must have been their home for years.

She was tiny, not even as tall as me, with short gray hair that curled in even rows around her head. As she reached close to me for an errant icicle, I caught a whiff of sweet perfume that made me remember another time.

There was crying then and hushed talking and lots of people when my father hadn't come back. He'd gone off across the fields as he had dozens of times before, but that time he had never returned.

I looked back out at the road while behind me Grandmother's voice went on softly. It didn't seem to matter to her whether I said anything or not, but I thought I should listen. So I turned my eyes from the road back to the tree.

"This dove was my mother's," Grandmother was saying as she carefully wrapped the glass bird in tissue paper. "It's been on every Christmas tree I can remember."

"It's pretty," I said, glad she'd been the one to remove it from the tree instead of me. Sometimes things seemed to just fall out of my hands no matter how careful I was. I reached for a felt Santa Claus face.

"Do you remember that one, Ance?" Grandmother asked. "You made it for me when you were in kindergarten."

I looked at the Santa Claus, but I didn't remember. "Do you know where all the ornaments came from, Grandmother?"

"Of course. Why put anything on a Christmas tree if it isn't special to you?"

As I stepped back to study the half-decorated tree with new eyes, it didn't look so shabby to me now. My father's Christmas trees must have looked a lot like this one when he was a boy growing up. I lifted off a tinfoil-wrapped cardboard star. "Did I make this, too?" I asked.

Grandmother took it from me as though it were as fragile as the glass dove. She stared at it a long time before she answered. "No, Russell made this. I thought sure this would be the year he'd come back." She glanced up at me. "You know, since you and your mother were here and all."

"Come back?"

She looked down at the star again. "Christmas would be a good time for him to remember and come back."

A funny little chill shook my insides. "How can Dad come back?" I said.

Grandmother didn't look up, but Grandfather stirred in his chair by the fire. "Come on, boy," he said as he stood up. "If you're going to be here for a year you might as well make yourself useful and help with the chores."

"But what about the tree?" I said.

"It'll still be here when we get back."

I looked at Grandmother, who had sunk down into one of the chairs by the stove with a faraway look on her face. She didn't even glance up as we left the room.

I followed Grandfather out through the kitchen to the back porch. His back was straight in spite of his years, but he dragged one of his feet as he walked. Mom had said that he'd had a slight stroke. When she had found that out, it had almost made her change her mind about leaving me here while she worked on an archaeology dig in Mexico, but there hadn't been any other relatives who could take me. I began to wish she'd looked into boarding schools.

Grandfather pulled a ragged denim work coat off a peg on the wall. After he buttoned it all the way to the top, he pulled on a hat and gloves. He never once really looked at me, more like over the top of my head as I shrugged on my jacket and waited for him to be ready to go.

"Ain't you got a hat, boy?" he asked.

"I don't need a hat. It's not that cold."

"Just like a city boy," Grandfather muttered as he went out the door. Once outside he moved faster than I expected, and I had to hurry to catch up.

"Grandfather," I said once I'd matched my stride to his. "What did Grandmother mean about my father coming back? He's dead. He can't come back."

Grandfather kept walking toward the barn without even glancing over at me, and a funny chill grew inside me as I began to wonder if he was going to ignore my question. I couldn't remember ever being alone with him before.

On our rare visits, Grandmother had fussed over me and Grandfather had rocked in his chair by the stove, only talking when Mom asked him something. Mom made excuses for him. She said it was his Indian blood that made him so quiet, and that though he didn't say much, when he did talk a person should listen. She said my father's dying had been especially hard on Grandfather, that it was hard on the both of them since Dad had been their only child and that we had to make allowances for them.

"Ruth watches too much television," Grandfather finally said as he pulled the barn door open. "Russ isn't ever coming back."

I didn't know what to say because something about the way he said it wasn't the way Mom talked about it. My father was dead. Mom had explained it to me every time I asked.

"Don't just stand there," Grandfather said. "We have to get the work done before nightfall."

I slipped in the door behind him. "Do you want me to carry in the wood?"

"Animals first." He picked up a bucket and filled it with corn out of a bin. "We don't have much stock anymore. Used to have all kinds—

horses, cows, sheep. But the last old ewe died last winter."

"What's the corn for then?"

"What do you use your eyes for, boy? Didn't you see the chickens?"

A few fat brown hens met us when we went back out of the barn. Grandfather gave me the bucket, and I scattered the kernels of corn on the ground by handfuls. If I was slow the hens rushed my feet and pecked at my shoelaces, which Grandfather thought was funny. When the bucket was empty we went back into the barn to feed the cat.

"Geraldine's a good mouser, but she doesn't take much to petting and such. So just set her feed out and let her be."

The big gray cat looked down from the loft at me, and I met her stare. She didn't jump down even after I set out the bowl of food for her, but that didn't bother me. We had made friends just by looking at each other. She'd let me rub her later.

"Just one more animal," Grandfather Sanford was saying.

"Jake?" I asked.

"You remember him then, do you?"

Of course I remembered the old red hound with the skin that seemed to be about to fall down across his eyes all the time. While I loved animals of all kinds, I especially loved dogs. That had been one of Mom's best selling points about my year with Grandmother and Grandfather Sanford, that maybe I could have a dog while I was here. She hadn't made any promises, but she'd said that when she came back from her dig in Mexico we'd try to find an apartment that allowed pets.

Jake came out of the woodshed to meet us, his tail slowly swaying back and forth in between steps. He moved stiffly, painfully.

"What's the matter with you, boy?" I scratched the wrinkled skin on his head, and he wagged his tail a bit faster.

"He's old," Grandfather said shortly.

"He wasn't that old the last time we were here." I pulled the hound's ears through my fingers.

"Dogs age fast." Grandfather leaned over slowly to pick up the dog's feeding pan. He grimaced with pain when he straightened back up. "Even faster than people do."

Taking the pan from Grandfather, I filled it from the sack on the shelf and set it down in front of Jake. The old dog crunched a couple of nuggets and then turned slowly to find his bed in the soft hole of dirt and wood shavings. He didn't even raise his head when I kept rubbing him.

"Don't pester him, boy," Grandfather said.

I stood and looked down at the old hound. "But I thought me and Jake would be able to walk in the woods together."

"You can take to the woods if you've a mind to, but Jake's roaming days are over. I don't look for him to live out the cold weather."

I looked out the shed door toward the trees in

the distance. Coyote Point was through there a mile or more away, and I'd been anxious to explore it all with Jake. Now it looked like if I went, I'd have to go alone.

"Do you think, Grandfather, that maybe . . ." I stopped, not sure of how to go on.

"Spit it out, boy, It's cold out here."

"Do you think that maybe, if you knew somebody who had one that they wanted to get rid of, that I could get a puppy while I was here? I mean I'd take care of it and everything."

"Jake here is too old to fool with a young pup bothering him," Grandfather said.

"Well, I just thought, I mean Mom said maybe it would be okay with you." I looked down at the ground.

"She shouldn't have made no promises to you like that."

"She didn't promise. She just said maybe." I rubbed a little ditch in the dirt with the toe of my shoe.

"Your mother should know your grandmother's too old to be worrying about a pup digging up her flowers and such." Grandfather looked at the house and then at me. "She must have taken leave of her senses telling you something like that."

He picked up a couple of pieces of wood and shuffled toward the back porch. After a minute, I loaded my arms and followed him. I was glad when he went on into the house and let me finish filling the woodbox by myself.

I carried in the loads of wood slowly, stopping

occasionally to talk to old Jake. Sometimes the end of his tail thumped in the dirt, and sometimes it didn't.

When I had the woodbox piled too high to put another stick on it, I went back outside one more time anyway. I stared out at the trees all along the southwest horizon. The last time I'd been in those trees it had been with my father five years ago, but I still remembered our walks. He'd not only loved the woods, he'd studied them. Dad had been a research scientist. He told me once that meant he was always looking for a new answer to an old puzzle.

Now as I stared at the trees with darkness falling around me, I missed him as I hadn't for years.

I went back to rub Jake's head one more time, but he was asleep and didn't open his eyes even after I touched him. I wanted to believe Grandfather would change his mind about the pup, but then I decided I shouldn't ask him to. Maybe he and Grandmother were too old to put up with another dog. Maybe they were too old to put up with me.

I stood up with a sigh. Whether they were too old or not, I was here.

The year stretched endlessly out in front on me. On Monday I'd have to start a strange school. Then at the end of every day, I'd have to come back here to a place where I was too young. Even the things I'd brought with me looked wrong and out of place in the room that had been my father's.

Suddenly I felt something warm wrapping around my leg. The cat had come from the barn to wind in and out between my legs, and I reached down to touch her softly behind the ears. "Thank you, Geraldine."

Then I went back into the house where the tree, bare of ornaments, was waiting for me to carry it out.

CHAPTER 2

I'd forgotten how quiet it could be in the woods, or maybe I had never known since this was the first time I'd been in the woods alone.

Grandmother Sanford hadn't wanted to let me go alone this time. "Now you wouldn't want to go over there by yourself," she'd said when I'd first asked if I could walk to Coyote Point. "You'll have to get a friend to go with you."

"I don't know anybody around here yet," I said.

"But you'll make friends soon," Grandmother said.

"Let the boy go." Grandfather spoke up from his chair by the fire. "The best way to see Coyote Point for the first time is alone."

Grandmother looked over at Grandfather. "But he might get lost like, like . . ."

"Russell never got lost." Grandfather turned to me. "You know the way, boy?"

"I can find it." I sounded surer than I felt.

Grandfather almost smiled. "Maybe you can."

"You could go with him, Emmett," Grandmother said.

"No." Grandfather opened the stove and shoved another piece of wood into the flames before he settled back in his rocker.

After looking at him a moment, Grandmother went out to the kitchen while I stood awkwardly by the stove, not sure what to do.

"Well, go on, boy," Grandfather finally said. "But be back in time to do your chores."

"I will," I promised.

In the kitchen Grandmother was standing at the stove staring at the empty pan she held. I hesitated, then said, "I won't get lost."

She didn't seem to hear me as she said softly, "I shouldn't have asked him to go with you. He wants to, you know. He used to go nearly every day, but since he was sick, he can't walk that far." She shook herself a little and looked around at me. "Now you pay attention to where you're walking, Ance, so that you can find your way back."

She made me pull a sock hat down over my head and put on gloves, but at last I got away from her out the back door. As I headed across the field toward the trees, I felt like I'd shrugged off a heavy coat, and now I was so light I practically floated above the ground.

I didn't find Coyote Point that day, and the next day I had to start school. It was different from my school back in the city but not so bad, and I had a couple of hours after school before chore time when I got to take to the woods. Finally, after a week of exploring, I found a faint path running through the trees and followed it straight to the Point.

Grandfather was right. When I walked out on the rocky point and looked down at the creek cutting through the narrow valley far below, I felt like the first person ever to stand there. Behind me, my tracks were the only marks in the light dusting of snow that had fallen earlier that day.

But then as I walked around the top of the cliff to find a way to the bottom, I spotted other tracks in the snow. Animal tracks. I wasn't really alone. Animals were all around me.

Stopping, I searched through the trees and bushes along the Point with my eyes. Nothing moved, but they were there. This was a place for animals, far removed from man. It had even been named for an animal. I stared back at the highest point on the cliff and imagined a coyote on the slab of rock howling into the night.

Just below the lip of the cliff, I crouched down in the snow and made myself as still as the boulder I leaned against, while down in the valley below, the creek gurgled and gushed around and over the rocks. After a while a brown mouse slipped out of a narrow crack in the cliff and moved to the right, then to the left before he lifted his nose and noticed me there in front of him. But he didn't run away.

He studied me, and I studied him. Then he scurried past me onto a fallen tree. Even when

I stood up he didn't slide under the rotting tree to hide.

Animals had never been really afraid of me. I'd been feeding the squirrels at the university from my hand ever since I could remember. Of course the squirrels on the campus were used to people. I wished I had a crumb of something to offer the mouse to see if he'd take it from me, but I didn't.

With a farewell glance at the mouse, I began down the steep path to the bottom of the cliff. I wondered how many other animals were watching me, not as ready to trust as the mouse. Rabbits, owls, deer, foxes. Maybe there were coyotes still around here.

As I looked up and around quickly, my boot skidded on the loose rock on the path. I slipped several feet before I could dig my heel against a root and stop myself. After that, I stepped more carefully, but I still half slid down the hill.

Near the bottom, rocks the size of small cars blocked the path. Looking up at the cliff, I could see the fresh gash of dark gray where the rock had recently parted from the wall. The fallen rocks, big as they were, didn't hide the yawning hole at the bottom of the cliff.

I had forgotten about the cave, but when I scooted across the boulders and down the incline into the opening, it was like going back in time. I'd been here before with Dad. I could remember sitting in the cool air of the cave while Dad explained how caves were formed.

"Caves are funny," he said. "Take this one.

Here the front of it's big enough to put a house in, and yet a few feet back from the entrance it peters out to a hole a coyote couldn't get through."

"Does it go on?"

"I think it could. This area is bound to be riddled with caves and someday I'm going to find a way into them."

It was odd how his long-forgotten words echoed so clearly in my mind now as I sat there in the cave entrance with the cold of the rock soaking through my jeans. Being on the farm and in the woods kept bringing back memories of my father, memories that set off a strange yearning inside me that I couldn't make go away or even understand.

When I came out of the cave entrance, I looked longingly at the creek that wound out of sight between the steep hillsides, but I turned back up the cliff path. It would be dark soon, and I still had my chores to do.

I moved quickly along paths through the trees that were more familiar every day, not because of the few times I'd walked them in the past week, but because my memories of my walks with my father were growing so much stronger.

Though it was near dark when I went in the house, Grandfather only looked up at me and said, "So you found it. Took you long enough."

"I'm sorry I'm late," I said. "I'll get right to the chores."

"I did the chores already. Hens go to roost when it starts getting dark."

"Oh." I looked down at my feet. "I'm sorry."

Grandfather's rocker creaked as he leaned back. After a long minute, he asked, "How did it look, boy?"

I remembered how I'd felt standing on top of Coyote Point looking down at the creek and valley below. "It was better than I remembered."

"Some things you just can't keep in your mind as good as they really are." Grandfather stared out the window behind me as though he could see past the barn and through the trees to the cliff. "You make sure you respect it."

"Respect it?"

"That's what I said. Respect it. Don't hurt it in any way and don't let it hurt you." His eyes came away from the window back to me. "Now you'd better get on out to the kitchen and tell your grandmother you're back. She has a way of worrying whether there's any need to or not."

I started to apologize again when I went into the kitchen, but Grandmother rushed in ahead of my words. "Where have you been, Rusty? Don't you know it's dark out there already?"

"Rusty?" I said while that funny little chill woke inside me.

Grandmother stopped fussing and stared at me. "Did I call you that?" She half laughed. "That's what I used to call your daddy when he was a boy. I guess you looked so much like him when you came in then that I just forgot."

"Do I really look like Dad?"

"Of course you do. You've always looked like

him from the time you were born. You have the Sanford mark on you."

"Then I look like Grandfather, too."

"Well, I suppose. You've got the same reddish hair your grandfather had when I met him. I mean here all he wanted to talk about was his Indian blood and he had this red hair and green eyes."

"I guess he wasn't all Indian."

"No, but he didn't want to talk about that. I think if he could have his way, he'd send progress packing and move time back to when the Indians owned these lands." She smiled a little and glanced toward the living room. "That's sort of what he's trying to do with Coyote Point over there. When his daddy died, he just gave that whole part of the farm back to nature, quit cutting wood off it or hay. He wouldn't even let the sheep graze over there."

"I'm glad."

"Why? If the sheep had eaten up a few of those bushes, it'd make walking easier."

"Walking isn't that hard."

Grandmother laughed. "No doubt about it. You're a Sanford through and through." From the living room, the sound of the stove door slamming shut made her smile disappear. "It about killed Emmett when he went over there after he had his stroke and got lost. He said he never did get to the Point."

"I could take him over there."

"No, that wouldn't be a good idea. At least not till he's stronger." She turned back to the stove to stir the stew she was cooking. "Why don't you go on and wash up, Ance, and then you can set the table for me."

I was to the door when she said, "And I really called you Rusty, did I? Won't your daddy laugh when we tell him about that when he comes home?"

She was smiling a little and shaking her head as though what she'd just said was as normal as could be. The funny little chill grew so strong inside me that I couldn't keep from shivering.

After a minute I made myself ask, "What do you mean, Grandmother? How could my father come back?"

She looked up at me as though surprised at my question. "Why, that would be easy enough. He'd maybe get hit on the head again or maybe he'd just remember all at once. I read about that happening to this man just the other day in one of my magazines. And he'd been gone over ten years. Then one day something happened and he just all of the sudden remembered his old name. He went home, and there was his wife still waiting for him at the same place they'd always lived."

It took me a minute to figure out what she meant. "You think Dad had amnesia?"

"Of course he has amnesia. Why else do you think he'd go away like that?"

"Mama said he was dead."

She didn't act like she heard me. "He must have fallen and hit his head that day. It happens all the time." She sneaked a look toward the living room and lowered her voice. "Emmett doesn't believe it, but I know Russell wouldn't have just gone off like that without telling anybody. He had to have hit his head."

The kitchen had gotten very hot while we talked. So hot that I felt a little dizzy. I shrugged off the coat I was still wearing, but that didn't seem to help much. "I'd better go wash up," I muttered and escaped to the bathroom.

I soaped and rinsed my hands thoroughly. Then I washed them again, but I couldn't wash my hands all night. While I was drying them, I caught sight of my face in the mirror over the sink. When I moved up and back, the wavy lines of the old mirror pulled my face out of shape just like an amusement park mirror. I knew there was one spot where the image in the mirror wasn't distorted, but tonight I couldn't seem to find that spot.

Where was Mom when I needed her? She could make some sense of all this. But she was thousands of miles away digging in the ground for ancient relics.

Grandmother had already set the table when I finally went back to the kitchen, and Grandfather was at his place at the head of the table, waiting.

I tried to listen to Grandmother as she kept up a steady stream of talk while we ate. I answered when I thought I should and kept quiet the rest of the time, but inside I felt funny, as if my whole life had bent out of shape like the image of my face in the bathroom mirror.

After supper, I was glad for the chore of taking out the potato peelings to dump where the hens could find them the next morning. It was good to be out in the dark of the night even if the cold did bring on a few shivers. At least these were real shivers, and not the shivers that inched up and down inside me when Grandmother talked about my father coming back.

Could she be right? Could it be that my father wasn't dead? But my mother would have never told me that if it hadn't been true. Still there must be something my mother hadn't told me, something I needed to know.

There had been something odd about Dad dying. Something mysterious that had never been explained. Even Mom, though she had always told me Dad was dead, had never really explained what had happened to him. Why hadn't I wondered about that before now?

A lonesome wind picked up and whirled some of the powdery snow up around me. Then Geraldine came out of the barn and began wrapping her body around my legs.

When I leaned over to stroke her from her head to the tip of her tail, she arched her back in pleasure. "You'll get your feet cold, girl," I said. "But I'm glad you came out."

Purring in answer, she pushed her head into my hand for another head-to-tail stroke. All at once she stiffened under my hand as from the distance there came the sound of a howl.

"What's the matter, girl? That's just an old dog somewhere." But then the sound came again, and it didn't sound like any dog I'd ever heard before. I stayed still listening for a long time, so long that Geraldine gave up hopes of any more rubbing and went back to the warmth of the barn, and my teeth began chattering so loudly that I wasn't sure I'd be able to hear the howl if it did come again.

When I went in, I stood with my back against the stove to warm. Grandfather poked up the fire for me and said, "You should have worn a coat."

"I didn't think I'd be out there long, but Geraldine came out of the barn to get me to rub her."

Grandfather looked up at me. I remembered how he'd told me not to bother the cat, but he didn't say anything.

Grandmother hadn't come in from the kitchen yet to switch on the television, and the only sounds were the tick of the clock, the pop of the fire, and the creak of Grandfather's rocker.

The howl I'd just heard echoed in my mind. "Grandfather, are there coyotes at Coyote Point?"

"There used to be before the sheep farmers cleaned them all out. I didn't let them use their poisons and traps at Coyote Point, but they got rid of them all anyway."

"How long ago was that?"

"Long before your time."

"Did you ever see one? A coyote, I mean."

"Yep. When you know how to watch, you can

spot most any animal no matter how shy of man they are."

"Did Dad ever see one?"

"Russ didn't have the patience for animal watching. He was always on the move, looking for something new."

"But he liked the woods. I remember the way he used to tell me about the trees and the animals when I went on walks with him."

"Can you remember that far back?" Grandfather said.

"It wasn't so long ago."

"A long time." Grandfather stared at the stove.

"How did Dad die?" I asked after another silence.

"I don't know that he did," Grandfather said.

"What do you mean? Mom told me he was dead." Being out in the cold night air had settled things back in their right places, but now everything was falling out of shape again.

"If that's what she told you, that's what she wants you to believe."

"But it's the truth, isn't it?"

"You'll have to ask your mother that."

"But what do you believe?"

"I don't think about it."

Grandmother came into the room, drying her hands on her apron before she reached around to untie it. "Well, what's on television tonight, boys?"

"I've got homework," I said.

"Oh well, we don't have to turn on the television," Grandmother said.

"That's okay. My books are upstairs."

"Are you sure it's warm enough up there?"

"It's warm enough."

"It's a long way from the stove." Grandmother looked worried.

"The boy said it was warm enough," Grandfather said. "Turn on your program."

In my room I sat on the bed and looked around the room, Dad's room. The award he'd won in a high school essay contest was still hanging on the wall beside a finger painting he must have done in grade school. On the shelves were the trophies he'd won playing in sports, an ancient microscope, and a dozen rocks he'd no doubt brought home from the Point. Everything in here was old.

My eyes caught on my stereo, and I stared at the turntable with its dials and buttons and at the speakers spread out away from it. Back home in our apartment I'd switched on the stereo every time I'd come into my room, but since I'd been here, I hadn't turned it on once.

Yanking the plug out of the wall, I picked up the stereo and shoved it in the bottom of the closet. Then I sat back down on the bed. I'd been here a week. Mom wouldn't be back for forty-nine more weeks.

The sound of Grandmother and Grandfather's favorite game show drifted up the stairs to my room. Then from outside I heard the howl again. Opening the window a crack, I listened for a long time, but I heard nothing but the wind in the trees.

I told myself it was probably a dog, but I didn't want to believe that. I wanted to believe a coyote was standing on the Point calling to other coyotes.

I stood at the window a long time wondering if I could find the coyote in the woods. It was easier to think about that than all the questions about Dad that had been answered years ago, but now needed new answers.

CHAPTER 3

As the days passed, I started feeling out each new memory that came back of my father before I'd let myself think too much about it. If it was something about the time he had disappeared, I'd push it away, but if it was something about the woods, I'd let it come. I didn't want to think about the questions I couldn't answer.

Even when Grandmother called me Rusty a few more times, I just smiled and let it pass. She was trying so hard to make me a home there on the farm. It wasn't her fault that we didn't know each other or that she was so old and I was so young. It wasn't my fault, either, but I was having to try just as hard to fit into their routine at the farm.

But though I tried to be extra careful, I still broke a glass and a plate before the second week was out. Grandmother pretended not to care, but I could tell the dishes were old and special to her. Then the whole house had a way of shaking whenever I went up the stairs or crossed my room. Even the bed creaked and groaned every time I turned over.

I took to spending every moment I could outside in spite of the cold. If I wasn't in the woods, I was in the barn loft with Geraldine curled up in my lap.

Of course every morning I caught the bus to Springdale Middle School. After the first week, I knew enough people so that I had somebody to talk to at lunch and between classes, but the school was as much different from my old school as the farm was from our apartment.

Where here there were only a couple of hundred students, in the city we'd had over a thousand in the school. At Bates Junior High, I'd been on the academic team and the newspaper staff. Here there was no academic team or newspaper. Basketball was the big interest, and I'd never been very good at basketball.

So I just sort of slid back in the corner to wait while the year stretched long in front of me.

Every afternoon when I came in from the bus, Grandmother would have cookies set out on the table for me and the same question. "How was school?"

I always answered "Fine," so that she'd smile and go on about her chores.

On Thursday of the second week, a girl climbed down off the bus behind me. The bus driver didn't act like there was anything strange about that as he shut the door and drove away leaving the two of us standing there at the end of the lane.

I stared at her, and she laughed. "You should see the look on your face," she said.

I'd noticed her on the bus and in a few of my classes at school. She had dark brown eyes and long straight brown hair pulled back from her face and caught in clips behind her ears. Best of all, she always seemed to be smiling about something. On the bus a whole bevy of little kids fought for the privilege of sitting beside her. I didn't blame them.

She started up the lane, but I stood rooted to my spot until she looked over her shoulder and said, "Well, come on. Aunt Ruth will think we've been kidnapped or something."

"Aunt Ruth?" I said as I caught up with her. "Are we related?"

Again she laughed as she shook her head, making her long hair sway gently. "Nope, but we've been neighbors with Aunt Ruth and Uncle Emmett forever. Mama even named me after Aunt Ruth. Carrie Ruth."

As soon as she said her name, I remembered that Grandmother had talked about a Carrie Ruth, but I hadn't paid much attention. She was always talking about people I didn't know. I decided I'd have to start listening better. "My name's Ance," I said.

"Russell Ance Sanford, Jr.," she said. "I know all about you."

"Oh?"

"Sure. Aunt Ruth talks about you all the time. About how brilliant you are, how you were the youngest member on the academic team back at your old school, and that you aren't just smart but good-looking as well." She stopped and grinned at me. "In fact she made you out so all around wonderful that I've been putting off coming over to see Aunt Ruth and Uncle Emmett. I thought maybe I wouldn't know what to say to such a fantastic boy."

"So far you haven't had much trouble finding words."

She laughed and turned back toward the house. "I talk too much. It's one of my many faults."

We walked four or five steps in silence, but that seemed to be as long as she could keep from talking. She looked at me out of the sides of her eyes and said, "Are you really that brilliant?"

I shrugged a little. "Grandmothers have a way of being a little prejudiced when it comes to their grandsons."

"I'll bet you are really that smart. You look like you would be. Something about your eyes, as though they're just gobbling up everything you see."

"Are they gobbling you up?" I asked.

She blushed and so did I. "A little," she said shyly.

"Sorry." I turned my eyes to the ground.

"That's okay. I don't think you can help it." She waited till I looked up again before she said, "I guess you're finding school here in Springdale a little dull."

"It's not so bad."

"I mean the classes."

"Well, so far I haven't learned anything new, but there's always tomorrow."

As we passed the barn, Geraldine came out to meet me but stopped when she saw Carrie Ruth. I squatted down, and the cat inched forward until her head was in my hand.

"Geraldine likes you?" Carrie said. "I didn't think that cat liked anybody except Uncle Emmett."

I looked up at Carrie Ruth. "She likes you, doesn't she?"

"Ha," Carrie said. "I used to try to pet her, but the few times I managed to catch her I got scratched for my trouble."

"She'll let you rub her now if you want to," I said as I ran my hand down Geraldine's back.

"How do you know?"

"I just know."

Carrie stared at me a minute before she reached down to the cat. "If she scratches me, I'm going to be real mad."

Geraldine endured Carrie Ruth's strokes with grace, allowing her two before she turned away and retreated to the barn.

Carrie raised up and stared at her hand. "I don't believe it. She didn't scratch me."

"I told you she wouldn't."

"Yeah, you did." She gave me a funny look before she shook herself a little, pushed her hair back over her shoulders, and went on toward the back porch. As we reached the door, she said, "I'll bet Aunt Ruth made chocolate brownies with walnuts. They're my favorite."

"She knew you were coming?" I asked as I followed her onto the back porch.

"Of course she knew I was coming. I come every Thursday after school and help her with her housework and stuff and she's teaching me to knit. Today we're going to put her quilt in the frame. The one she's been piecing all winter."

"You didn't come last Thursday."

"I had a sore throat."

"You were on the bus."

"So, it wasn't that sore." She flipped around and went on into the kitchen ahead of me.

After hanging my coat up on the hook on the wall, I followed her. She hugged Grandmother while Grandfather stood in the doorway smiling at her. On the table there was a plate of chocolate brownies.

After we ate our snack, I helped them set up the quilting frames. Grandmother ran her hands along the smooth wooden poles and said, "I've made many a quilt on these, but it's always exciting putting in a new one."

"This has got to be the prettiest one you ever made." Carrie held up the quilt top. It was white with bright blue rings running through it. "It's the double wedding ring pattern," Carrie told me.

"Mom's got one almost like that at home," I said.

"That's right," Grandmother said. "I made Diane and Russell one when they married. Russell held it up at the shower and told me I was an artist. I wonder what he'd say about this one."

Tears sprang to Grandmother's eyes as she stared at the quilt while Grandfather began noisily poking up the fire. Carrie looked between them and then frowned at me over the quilt top she still held up. Her mouth straightened out as she loosely folded the quilt before she looked at Grandmother with a big smile and said, "We'd better get started on this or we won't get it in the frames before Mama gets here."

Grandfather eased back in his rocking chair, and Grandmother reached for her roll of quilt batting. The shadow of gloom melted away in the face of Carrie's smile. Except for around me. There the shadow lingered, bringing back all the questions I had been refusing to think about.

"I've got to do my chores," I said and went back out on the porch to get my coat.

Once outside I looked toward the woods that stood between me and Coyote Point and then at the sun which was already low in the sky. There wouldn't be time to go to the Point today. I'd wasted too much time talking to Carrie Ruth.

I glanced back toward the house and wondered what she would think if she knew I went over to the Point every day to sit like a stone for an hour while I let the animals get used to me. Already I'd seen a red fox, a rabbit, two squirrels, a hawk, and of course the little mouse. I hadn't seen a coyote, but I was sure there was one in the woods. And I was just as sure that he was watching me.

Sticking my hands in my pockets, I went on to the barn to get the corn for the hens who were following me. She'd laugh, I thought. Making friends with wild animals would seem strange to her. It seemed strange to nearly everybody. Even back home in the city, my friends had laughed at me when I fed the birds and squirrels on campus. As nice as Carrie Ruth's laugh was, I didn't think I wanted her to laugh at me trying to make contact with a coyote that I had never even seen.

When I thought about meeting the coyote, it did seem silly, but at the same time I knew I could do it. I was sorry it was too late to try today.

By the time I went back in, the quilt top was in the frames which filled up half the living room. Both Grandmother and Carrie Ruth with thimbles on their middle fingers were making stitches in and out of the tightly stretched material.

Carrie looked up at me with her wide smile. "Aunt Ruth says if I help quilt this one, she'll give it to me."

A few minutes later, Carrie's mother stopped to pick her up on her way home from her job at the doctor's office in Springdale. When Carrie introduced me to her, she said, "Of course I remember Ance. But you were just a little boy the last time I saw you. How long ago has that been?"

Grandmother looked up from her seat by the quilting frames. "I imagine it was about five years ago. That's when Russell went away, you know."

As she glanced over at my grandmother, a soft look of pity came into Mrs. Kenton's eyes that not even her bright smile could hide when she looked back at me. "It's so nice to have you back here for a while, Ance."

When I just nodded a little, she kept talking. "And imagine your mother becoming an archaeology professor and now going off on a dig. I guess she's got more nerve than most of us. Have you heard from her since she left?"

"Not yet, but she said she'd call if she could."

The pity grew in Mrs. Kenton's eyes even while she said, "I'm sure she'll call soon."

The next day Carrie got off the school bus at the farm again. "Aunt Ruth says I'll need to come every day I can to help with the quilt. I hope you don't mind."

"Why should I mind?"

"Oh, I don't know." Carrie hitched her load of schoolbooks up closer to her. "I thought maybe I'd be in your way or something. I mean you looked sort of upset when I was leaving yesterday."

"I wasn't upset."

"Yes, you were. You were upset by Mama and what she said about your mother calling you."

I didn't have any books, and as I watched Carrie shift hers from one arm to the other, I thought I should offer to carry her books. But since we were already halfway to the house, I only shoved my hands in my pockets and said, "I don't like for people to feel sorry for me."

"Mama can't help it. And sometimes she says more than she should, but I guess everybody around here has always talked about the Sanfords. I guess they always will."

"Why?"

"First off, Uncle Emmett and his Indian blood. Uncle Emmett has done some pretty strange things."

"What do you mean? Strange things?"

"Oh, I don't know. All kinds of stuff. Folks used to come get him to help with their cows and horses after the vets would give up on them, and somehow Uncle Emmett could make them live. He has a way with animals. They say that once when he was a boy he made a pet of a wolf. Of course now what they talk about most is the way he is about Coyote Point."

"He just wants to protect it, keep it natural."

"I suppose, but most of the farmers around here think not working that much land is a little strange. And then there was your father." She stopped before she got to the porch and looked sideways at me. "He was brilliant, too. They say he might even have discovered the cure for cancer if he'd had enough time."

"I guess they talk about how he disappeared, too." I looked off at the trees.

"Yes."

"Grandmother thinks he has amnesia."

"I know." She was quiet for a minute before she asked, "What do you think?"

"I don't have to think. I know. He's dead."

"But his body was never found."

I looked at her. That was the part I'd forgotten or maybe I'd never known. "What do you mean his body was never found?"

"Just that. They never found his body. You knew that, didn't you?"

"Of course I did," I said quickly. "But that doesn't mean he's not dead." I wished we hadn't started talking about Dad. "Mom said he was dead, and she wouldn't have told me that unless she was sure it was true."

"I suppose not," Carrie said. Then as if she couldn't keep from saying it, she went on. "But your mother never remarried."

"So? What difference does that make?" I stared at Carrie.

She looked down at her books. "I don't know. Maybe just that she's not so absolutely sure after all."

"That's crazy."

"Yeah, it probably is." Carrie looked up at me. "Look, I'm sorry, Ance. Like my mother, I say more than I should sometimes."

"Yeah."

Carrie tried to laugh, but the sound was all wrong. "Let's go in and see what kind of goodies Aunt Ruth has fixed for us today."

"You go ahead." I let my eyes drift back to

the trees beyond the barn. "And tell Grandmother I've gone for a walk, but I'll be back in time to do my chores."

She touched my arm before I could turn away. "You're not mad at me, are you, Ance?"

"I'm not mad," I said and left her there at the door while I crossed the field in a direct line toward Coyote Point.

Since the ground was frozen, I didn't have to worry about getting my school shoes muddy. But even if I'd had to wade in mud, I'd still have had to go. I couldn't go in the house with Carrie and eat Grandmother's cookies. I needed to think.

But once I picked a spot on top of Coyote Point and settled down to watch the animals, I did my best not to think. Still nothing, not so much as my friend, the mouse, poked out of the bushes where I could see it.

When my hands and feet began to stiffen and ache from the cold, I stood up and began the walk back to the house. Carrie's mother should have come for her by now.

I was almost out of the trees when the coyote stepped out in the path about twenty-five feet in front of me. At first I thought I must be downwind of him, and he didn't know I was there. But then he turned slowly to face me.

He was smaller than I expected, not much bigger than a fox. Although the rest of his coat mingled light brown, gray, and black, the hair around his ears was almost as red as mine.

He stared at me with glittering yellow eyes for a few seconds before he slipped back into the bushes and disappeared almost immediately.

CHAPTER 4

When Mom finally called that night, I had my questions ready, but they were harder to ask than I'd thought they'd be.

After Grandmother handed me the phone, she'd hovered nearby, listening. She didn't leave me alone to talk to Mom until Grandfather called from the kitchen that her beans were burning.

Picking up the phone, I carried it as far as the cord would reach into the hallway out of the living room. Mom was telling me about how they were gathering their supplies and that they'd be leaving for the dig the next morning. She'd waited till now to call to give me time to adjust to the farm.

When she finished telling me all that, a small silence fell between us. "You're not saying much, Ance," she said. "Is everything all right on the farm? Your grandmother and grandfather are well, aren't they?"

"They're okay," I said. "Old but okay, I guess.

But Mom, everything's pretty weird around here."

"Weird? What do you mean by that?" Her voice sounded tight all of the sudden.

I knew she didn't really want to hear that anything was wrong, but I had to have answers. "It's about Dad."

The sound of Mom's sigh whispered along the miles of telephone lines to me. "What about him?"

"Grandmother keeps calling me Rusty."

"Well, that's not so bad. You can put up with that."

"It makes me feel funny."

"It's what she called your father when he was a boy."

"That's what she said. But Mom, she keeps talking about when Dad comes back. He can't come back, can he, Mom?"

"Of course not. Your father's dead."

"Grandmother doesn't believe that, and I'm not sure Grandfather does, either."

"I know," Mom said softly.

I waited for her to go on, to explain, but she didn't. Finally I broke the uneasy silence between us. "Tell me what happened to Dad."

"Ask your grandfather."

"He won't tell me anything. I don't think he likes me very much."

"Oh, Ance," Mom said. "Why would you say a thing like that?"

"I don't know."

"He might not be feeling good and that might

be making him cross, but of course he likes you."

"I guess so," I said. "But Mom, I've got to know what happened to Dad."

"I don't have time to go into all that on the phone. The rest of the group is outside waiting on me."

I didn't say any more as I listened to the hum of the telephone in my ear.

After a few seconds, Mom cleared her throat and said, "Well, then, how's school?"

"Fine."

"Really? Have you learned anything yet?"

"Not yet, but there's always tomorrow." The line had worked with Carrie. Maybe it would with Mom.

It did. She laughed. "Oh, Ance." Then the laugh was gone, and she said, "I miss you, honey."

"Yeah, I miss you, too."

There was some kind of noise in the background. "Look, Ance, I've got to go. And don't worry about all that other stuff. I'll write you a letter."

The line went dead before I could say goodbye. When I carried the phone back in the living room and put it on the table, Grandfather looked up at me, but he didn't say anything.

"She's okay," I said.

"I figured she was," he said.

"They were getting ready to go out wherever the dig is."

Grandfather made a sound in his throat that could have meant anything.

I looked away from him to the quilt in the frames. "She's going to write me a letter."

"That's sensible," Grandfather said. "Phone calls from way off down there are bound to be expensive."

I went over to stand by the stove. In the kitchen I could hear Grandmother putting supper on the table, but I didn't go in to help her. Instead I just stood there and listened to the fire pop and the old clock tick on the mantle behind the stove.

To keep from thinking about how I still didn't have any answers, I thought about how the coyote's eyes had looked as he'd stared at me. There'd been no fear in those golden eyes, only curiosity as he'd sized me up. Had I passed his inspection?

"Have you ever known anybody who had a coyote for a pet?" I asked Grandfather.

"I have," Grandfather said. "A cruel thing to do to the animal."

"Why?" I looked at Grandfather, but he was staring at the stove.

"A wild animal needs to be free. Not penned up in a yard somewhere."

I remembered what Carrie had said about Grandfather. "But didn't you have a pet wolf once?"

"I knew a wolf. He wasn't my pet," Grandfather said crossly.

"What do you mean when you say you knew him?"

Grandmother called from the kitchen that supper was ready, and Grandfather heaved himself out of the chair. Standing there beside me, he looked straight into my eyes and said, "If a person doesn't know already there's no way of explaining it to them."

Ten days passed before I got Mom's letter. During that time I spent every free moment in the woods trying to find the coyote, but I didn't see him again. I found his tracks once when we had an inch of snow. I tried to follow them, but they kept turning back and twisting around until it was impossible to figure out the main trail.

I wanted to ask Grandfather about tracking. I was sure he'd be able to tell me how to stay on the true trail, but whenever he and I were alone, I could never find the right words for my questions. He didn't encourage any kind of talking, much less questions.

Except when Carrie was there. She came nearly every day to work on the quilt, and while she was there, the house was never quiet or gloomy. She could even make Grandfather laugh.

She and Grandmother talked me into trying my hand at stitching a square of the quilt, but my hands turned all thumbs when I took hold of the needle. Carrie laughed so much watching me that she cried and had to stop working on the quilt herself so her tears wouldn't spot the cloth.

Grandmother took up for me. "Now, Ance is growing and that makes a boy a mite clumsy," she said. But the next day when I passed the quilt, I saw she had picked out my irregular stitches and replaced them with her neat, even ones.

Mom's letter came on a Monday afternoon. It was in the mailbox waiting for me when Carrie and I got off the bus. Although Carrie was waiting for me to come back across the road and start up the lane with her, I stood there staring at the Mexican stamp and the strange postmark for a long time. Until that moment, I hadn't realized just how far away Mom was.

Carrie couldn't stand it. She came across the road to peek at the letter I held. "What is it?" she asked.

"A letter from Mom." I stuffed it in my coat pocket.

"Aren't you going to open it?" Carrie asked.

"Not here in the middle of the road."

She didn't say any more about the letter till we were halfway up the lane. "It was funny-looking, wasn't it? Your mom's letter. I don't guess I've ever seen a letter from another country. Imagine having to put U.S.A. in the address." She hesitated before she asked, "Can I see it again?"

Reluctantly I pulled the envelope out of my pocket and held it out to her. "I'll bet she's having fun," she said as she studied the front of it.

"She said it would be a lot of hard work."

"But fun, too," Carrie repeated, handing the letter back to me. "I admire her."

"Why?"

"Oh, I don't know, I guess because she's out there doing something important. Making new discoveries. It has to be exciting."

"I don't know whether she's made any discoveries."

"She might tell you about it in the letter."

"She might." I shoved the letter back in my pocket. "I hope she's not having too much fun."

"Why?"

"She might not want to come back at the end of the year, and I might be stuck here forever."

"Would that be so bad?"

"It wouldn't be too good. I don't think Grandmother and Grandfather are ready to take on a permanent grandson. I'm not sure they're going to be able to put up with me for a year."

"Don't be silly. Aunt Ruth looked forward to your coming for months. That's all she talked about, and Uncle Emmett feels the same even if he doesn't act like it sometimes."

"I think I'm more trouble than either of them bargained for."

Carrie stopped at the yard gate and stared at me. "What trouble are you?"

"Oh, I don't know."

"Yes, you do. You just don't want to tell me what you're really thinking. Maybe you think I'm too dumb to understand."

"I don't think you're dumb," I said. When she

just glared at me, I went on. "Okay. I think maybe I make them think too much about my father."

She raised her eyebrows at me. "Maybe it's the other way around. Maybe being here is making *you* think too much about your father."

"How could I think too much about him? I just want to know what happened to him."

"Then find out," she said as she turned and went on into the house.

The letter burned in my pocket, but I didn't pull it out to read until after I'd eaten Grandmother's brownies and was sitting on the rock at Coyote Point.

The day was cloudy and cold with a few snowflakes flying in the air, but I wasn't worried about the weather. With hands that weren't shaking from the cold, I pulled Mom's letter out and tore it open.

I skimmed through the first part where she wrote about the dig and the weather and her coworkers. Finally on the second page, I found what I was looking for:

> I promised to tell you about your father's death, Ance, so I will though I don't like to think about it. I should have talked to you about it before I took you to the farm. I'm sorry.
>
> You know your father was a scientist, and a very good one. He had a way of seeing everything in a clear, fresh light unhindered by accepted ideas. He liked his work in the lab-

oratory, but he needed time away from it, too. To rest his mind, he said.

Yet he never really got away from the scientist in himself. At the farm, the woods around Coyote Point became his laboratory. No matter what the weather, he went out every day just like a kid anxious to make some new discovery, whether it was a new fossil or a plant or bird he'd never seen before. Sometimes your grandfather went with him, and sometimes he took you. Do you remember? You were so little when he first took you into the woods that I worried you'd wander away from him and get hurt. Coyote Point is a beautiful place, but wild and dangerous, too. But I never worried about Russell. Never.

I looked up from the letter and down at the narrow valley far below me while the brisk wind tugged at the pages of my mother's letter. With her words fresh in my mind, I almost scooted back from the edge of the cliff.

But I sat still. The rock was broad, flat, and bedded firmly in the ground. I held down the edges of Mom's letter and began reading again.

The day he disappeared, he left the house early. We were going home the next day, and he wanted to spend as much of the day as he could in the woods. Your grandmother and I watched him walk across the fields from the window. She laughed and said, "I don't know what Rusty expects to find out in those woods, but he's been looking for it since he was knee-high to a grasshopper." Your grandmother and I were so close then, maybe because we both loved your father so much.

It started out a beautiful day, the sun shining, only a few soft clouds, but by noon the clouds were thick and black. The rain started in the early afternoon and came down in torrents. Your grandmother got worried first, jumping up to peek out the window every few minutes. By five o'clock when the rain had begun to let up, we were all worried although none of us said so, not even when your grandfather put on his raincoat and left without a word.

Shivering, I pulled my coat closer around me, but I didn't take my eyes off the words on the paper.

He came back an hour after dark alone. They had search parties out the next day and for days after that, but I knew they wouldn't find anything if Emmett Sanford couldn't. He stayed out practically day and night, but there was nothing to be found. Your father had disappeared.

I turned the page over, no longer feeling the wind, no longer caring about the view below me.

So you see I have no sure answer to your question of what happened to your father. We all came up with our different answers. Your grandmother clutched at the wild story that Russell hit his head and had amnesia. I didn't think she still believed that after all these years. I'm not sure what your grandfather believes, but he kept searching for months after we came back to the city.

I know Russell is dead. I knew that the first day when Father Sanford came home alone. I don't know how he died, but I always believed he drowned. You know that creek at Coyote Point? Russell liked to follow its flow down to the river. Maybe that day he lost his footing or the floodwaters swept him away or maybe something else happened. I don't know. I just know he's dead, and it's best if we accept that and not think too much about what we can't know. After all this time, I doubt if we'll ever know exactly what happened.

She switched off to questions about school and I folded the letter and stuffed it back in my pocket. I'd read the rest later.

Slowly I stood up and stared down at the creek far below as if somehow the bare limbs of the trees and the gray rocks might give me an answer. But there was no answer. My father had disappeared. No one knew what had happened to him.

The walk back through the woods was long and cold. The wind had picked up and carried flurries of snow that stung my face. I kept my eyes on the ground, hardly looking at the trees beside me. That's why I nearly missed seeing the little rabbit.

He was hunkered down under a bush, and when I strayed off the path, I almost stepped right on top of him. He didn't jump away but only stared at me while he awaited his fate.

Dropping down on the ground in front of the animal, I carefully examined him with my eyes. His ears and nose twitched, but he sat still till I began to reach toward him. When he tried to dodge sideways, one of his back legs hung uselessly behind him.

I stayed still until the rabbit looked at me again. "You can trust me," I said softly. I stared at him a long time before I touched the rabbit's fur. A slight shiver ran through him, but he didn't try to escape my hold.

As I began the walk on toward the house with the rabbit tucked inside my coat, a hawk rose out of the tree to my left and soared away with a high-pitched whistling scream. I had taken his meal.

CHAPTER 5

Back at the barn I put the rabbit in the feed bin before I went to the house for Grandfather. Carrie had said he could help animals.

Grandfather frowned, but he got up from his rocking chair and put on his hat and coat.

"Geraldine will have him by now," he said as we went across the yard.

"I put him in the bin." I looked over at Grandfather. "Do you think you can help him?"

"Can't say until I see him, but you should have left him there."

"If I had, the hawk would have gotten him."

"More reason than ever you should have let the animal be," Grandfather said shortly. "Hawks eat rabbits. That's the way of things over at the Point, and you aren't meant to interfere with that way."

In the barn I reached into the bin and lifted the rabbit out. "Do you want me to take him back?" I asked as I stroked the rabbit's soft fur. "Put him back where he was?"

"Too late now to undo what's been done. The hawk's either gone to his roost hungry or found another supper." He held out his hands. "Let me have the animal."

Grandfather's hands gentled as he took the rabbit and began making a low crooning noise in the throat. The rabbit didn't jerk once, not even when Grandfather pulled on his leg.

Out of nowhere Geraldine appeared and pounced up on the feed bin to stare at the rabbit. Grandfather glanced up at her. "Never mind, Miss Kitty."

Geraldine's tail flicked back and forth, and the rabbit jerked for the first time since Grandfather had taken hold of him. To me Grandfather said, "Go feed Geraldine before she forgets her manners. Then get at the rest of your chores. It's almost dark."

"But what about the rabbit?"

"I'll take care of the rabbit." He began making the crooning noise again.

I ran through my chores, scaring the hens into a fit of clucking and hardly pausing long enough to pet old Jake on the head, but still Grandfather was through working on the rabbit's leg before I got back to the barn. The rabbit, who sat in the middle of the floor, took a hesitant jump when I came in the door.

"What was wrong with him?" I asked.

"A bone out of joint."

"What do you think happened to him?"

"Couldn't say. I didn't see it."

"But you must have some kind of idea what might have happened," I insisted.

"I could make up a story to tell you, but that doesn't mean it'd be the truth," Grandfather said. "Only a story."

Both of us watched the rabbit as he gingerly began moving around on the floor. "He's not afraid of us," I said.

Grandfather looked up at me sharply. "Did he fight you when you first picked him up?"

"No."

Grandfather kept looking at me, but he didn't say any more. After a minute I shoved my hands in my pocket and felt my mother's letter. Still staring at the rabbit, I said, "I got a letter from Mom today."

"Carrie Ruth told us."

The wind pushed against the barn, sneaking through the cracks to make me shiver, and the hard, icy bits of snow peppering against the roof seemed to make the silence inside that much louder.

My voice shook a little as I broke that silence. "She thinks my father drowned."

"I've heard her say as much."

"You don't believe it?"

"They dragged the river."

"You mean they didn't find his body?" I said. "But they didn't find his body anywhere, and something had to have happened to him."

"Yep," Grandfather said as he looked around the room. "Get that crate over there and put the rabbit in it."

I didn't move from my spot. "What do you think happened to him?"

Grandfather went over, pulled the crate away from the wall, and carried it back to the rabbit, who had raised his head at the noise but didn't try to hop away when Grandfather reached down to catch him.

"What do you think happened to my father?" I repeated.

Grandfather settled the rabbit in the crate and without looking at me, answered, "I could make you up a story just like about this rabbit here, but that's all it would be. A story."

"But I've got to know."

"So did I, boy. So did I," Grandfather said softly.

Outside the wind calmed for a minute, and we could hear Grandmother calling us from the back door. "Tell me what you think, Grandfather," I begged.

Grandfather stared up at me, his eyes not really seeing me. "He didn't get lost. He didn't fall off the cliff, and he didn't drown."

"What then?"

"Who do you think I am? God with all the answers?" Grandfather said crossly.

I dropped my eyes to my feet. "No," I said softly.

"Good," Grandfather said. "Now grab hold of this box, and let's get to the house. Ruth gets cranky if she has to hold supper."

I picked up the crate. "Where do you want me to put it?"

"On the back porch. Ruth won't like it, but it can't be helped. This one here wasn't meant for Geraldine. Maybe a hawk's or a fox's meal, but not a cat's." He held the barn door open for me. "Tomorrow you'll have to take him back to the Point and turn him loose."

When I didn't say anything, Grandfather went on. "You weren't planning on keeping him, were you?"

"No, I just brought him in because he was hurt," I said as I went through the door out into the wind. I remembered how soft and warm the little rabbit had felt inside my coat, and I was glad for the cold wind that was hitting me in the face making my eyes water.

Grandmother stood in the kitchen door and watched us come in the porch. "What in the world have you got there?"

"It's a hurt rabbit the boy found over at the Point," Grandfather said.

"Now we can't be having rabbits in the house," Grandmother said. "You should have left him at the barn."

"Geraldine would get him," I said.

"Oh," Grandmother said.

"The boy's taking him back to the woods tomorrow."

"Then I guess it'll be all right just this once," she said. "You two come along now. Supper's getting cold." She went back into the kitchen.

I sat the crate down where Grandfather pointed, then shrugged off my coat and hung it up. Pulling Mom's letter out of the pocket, I folded it three times and stuffed it down in my jeans.

I was about to go in to wash up when Grandfather said, "About your father, boy." I stopped and waited. "He went away. He just went away. That's all any of us know."

I stared at Grandfather's back as he hung up his coat slowly. "You think he went away because he wanted to?"

"I don't think anything. I just know he's gone."

At supper Grandmother kept asking me what Mom had said in her letter, and I told her some things Mom had written about the dig and the house she was sharing with two other women. But though I tried, I just couldn't keep the talk going. Finally Grandmother gave up, and we ate the rest of the meal in silence.

Before breakfast the next morning, I went out on the back porch to check on the rabbit. He was sitting quietly in the box munching on a lettuce leaf.

"Did you feed the rabbit, Grandmother?" I asked when I went back in the kitchen.

"Not me," Grandmother said with a laugh. "Emmett must have fed him before he went to check on things at the barn. I used to try to feed Emmett's animals, but they were always afraid of me."

"What animals?"

Grandmother sat down at the table with me. "Years ago, Emmett used to bring in hurt animals all the time. Then one time a raccoon got loose, killed three chickens, and about bit your father's finger off when he tried to catch him and put him back up." Grandmother smiled. "Rusty is a lot like Emmett, but he never had his way with wild animals."

"Were Dad and Grandfather close?"

"Close? They were so close they could practically read one another's minds if they tried." Her eyes got watery. "Rusty can't know how much we miss him, or he'd come back."

I choked down my toast with a gulp of milk and jumped up from the table. "The bus'll be here in a few minutes."

She stared at the wall as if she hadn't heard me. "Bye, Grandmother," I said, and then as I passed her, I dropped an awkward kiss on her cheek.

"Goodbye, Rusty. You're going to have to run or you'll never make it in time."

I grabbed my coat off the peg and ran out the door. Although I knew I had plenty of time, I didn't stop running until I was at the end of the lane. Then I stood there panting, wishing I could keep running.

When I climbed on the bus, Carrie smiled at me, but even though she sat alone this morning, I still plopped down in the seat behind her.

She flipped her hair up and out of the way as she turned and said, "Well, had your mother made any new discoveries at her dig yet?"

For the first time I realized that I'd never finished reading my mother's letter. "No, I guess not," I said.

"Didn't she tell you?"

"She wrote more about what the place looked like. Where she was living and stuff like that."

"Tell me about that," Carrie said.

I told her some of the things Mom had written in the letter, but I was glad when a couple of Carrie's grade school admirers sat down beside her and took her attention away from me.

That afternoon I showed Carrie the rabbit before we went into the kitchen. "Grandfather fixed his leg," I said.

"Are you going to keep him for a pet?" Carrie leaned down for a better look at the rabbit. Trembling, he tried to hide in the corner of the box.

"He doesn't want to be a pet."

Carrie looked up at me. "How do you know?"

"Would you want to trade living in the woods over at the Point for a box like this?"

"I don't know. I've never been a rabbit, but at least he wouldn't have to worry about a fox getting him."

"Or a hawk or a coyote," I said.

"Coyote?" Carrie said. "There aren't any coyotes around here anymore."

"How can you be sure of that?"

"The farmers killed them all out years ago because they kill sheep."

"Surely some survived."

"Not around here, or at least that's what my father and Uncle Emmett say. They used to argue about coyotes when I was little, but it didn't really matter since all the coyotes were gone anyway."

"I thought I heard one howl the other night."

Carrie laughed. "How would you know it was a coyote? Aunt Ruth told me you've lived in the city all your life."

With a shrug, I looked away from her back to the rabbit. "I guess it could have been a dog."

Carrie's laugh died. I felt her eyes on me, but I wouldn't look at her. Finally she said, "When are you going to take the rabbit back?"

"As soon as I change into my old clothes."

Carrie stepped nearer the box. "Do you think he'd let me touch him?"

"No, it'd scare him too much."

"How come it doesn't scare him when you touch him then?"

"I don't know," I said as I pulled the top back over the box. "It just doesn't."

Grandmother came out on the porch to hurry us into the kitchen then, so Carrie just gave me a funny look and didn't say anything else.

Later I carried the rabbit back to the very tree stump where I had found him. When I put him down, he twitched his nose a couple of times, let his ears quiver in the wind, and then hopped off without a backward glance. Once he was safely hidden in some brush, I wanted to believe he turned back to look at me, but I couldn't see his eyes.

As I moved on toward the cliff, I heard the shrill whistle of the hawk somewhere off above the trees. I looked back toward the bushes where the rabbit had disappeared, but if he was still there I couldn't see him.

I didn't go back to check. I had kept the hawk from him once. I wouldn't do it again. Since Grandfather had fixed his leg, the animal still had a chance at survival.

It might have been fun to keep the rabbit, but when I remembered the box that would have been his home, I knew it was better the rabbit was free even if he had to take his chances with the hawk and even if I never knew what happened to him. The rabbit wouldn't remember me.

But I would remember the rabbit. In a way I had known him just as I knew the little mouse who often scurried around me when I sat down in his territory. I wanted to know all the animals at the Point like that. I wanted them to accept me and not be afraid of me.

Still even after I sat down and the mouse came close enough to sniff at my boot, I was lonely. Even if I got to know all the animals in the woods, none of them would miss me if I stopped coming. The little mouse wouldn't come out of his crack in the wall and wonder where I was.

They wouldn't wonder what had happened to me like I wondered what had happened to my father. I forgot about the rabbit and the hawk and the mouse and even about the coyote that Carrie had said couldn't be here.

For the first time since I'd come to the farm I thought hard about the day my father had disappeared. But no matter how hard I concentrated all I could remember was Mom staring out the window, Grandmother crying softly, and Grandfather coming in with water streaming off him unnoticed to make a puddle in the middle of the living room floor while he shook his head.

There had been talk then, questions, but I didn't remember what they were. There were still questions. Questions without sure answers although Mom, Grandmother, and Grandfather had each settled on a different answer. Only one answer could be the true answer. Could Grandfather be right—had Dad just walked away from us?

I thought back over the words of Mom's letter and the words she'd used to answer my questions about Dad in the past. It was possible that Dad could have died here at Coyote Point. As Mom said, it was a wild, dangerous place.

I looked at the cliff towering high into the air. One slip on the top of it and a person could fall to his death on the rocks below. Here and there around me were trees with the weathered scars of lightning hits. Down below I could see the huge rocks that had broken free from the cliff and crashed to the ground, and always there was the rush of the creek running along its path to the river. It was gentle, peaceful now, but a flash flood might change it to something else.

Still there should have been something to show what had happened to my father. People didn't just disappear.

I made myself think about the fact that maybe

Dad had simply gone away as Grandfather had said. I knew kids whose fathers had done that, but they talked to them. They knew where they were. They hadn't vanished without a trace.

I was so deep in thought that I didn't see the coyote until he was fully out in the open standing on the Point just as I'd imagined him the night I'd heard him howling. He lifted his nose high now, but he didn't howl. He only sniffed the air.

He seemed almost to pose there in front of me before turning slowly to let me know he knew I was there. I was well below the Point, and the coyote looked down at me. We stared at each other for a long time across the space separating us before he suddenly whirled and trotted off the rock.

For a minute I thought he might be coming closer, but then when I knew he was gone for the day, I stood up. I needed to be going, too.

As I walked back through the trees, memories of my father came to walk with me. He had never rushed me when we were in the woods, letting me explore anything that caught my interest. He wanted me to love Coyote Point as he did. Even Grandfather had been patient with me then, and both of them would search out things in the woods to share with me. Then if I got tired of walking, one of them would laugh and swing me up on his shoulders to ride high in the trees.

Thinking about it made me feel warm inside. Every time I remembered Dad it was with a smile on his face. He was happy. He wouldn't have gone away. Yet he was gone; so the questions remained.

I pushed them aside and thought instead about the coyote. I wanted to know him the way Grandfather had known his wolf.

CHAPTER 6

Early the next week a storm dropped twelve inches of snow on the farm. Drifts piled high as the fence posts in places, and school was closed until the roads could be cleared.

Carrie couldn't get through the snow up our lane to help Grandmother with the quilt. So Grandmother pushed the quilting frames back against the wall and started cutting pieces for a new quilt.

"It'll mean more to her if she helps quilt it all," Grandmother said. She held up a piece of green material to make sure she had the sides even and straight. "I'll make this one for you, Ance."

I looked up from my book. "Do I have to help quilt it?"

Grandmother laughed. "I don't think you were cut out for quilting. Maybe Carrie Ruth will help me with it, too."

"Maybe." I smiled at Grandmother.

"Carrie Ruth's such a sweet girl," Grandmother said. "You do like her, don't you, Ance?"

"Everybody likes Carrie," I said. "On the bus, the little kids fight over who gets to sit beside her."

Grandfather, who I had thought was napping in his chair, looked up and said, "You don't fight with them?"

"No," I said as my face warmed a little.

Grandfather laughed, the first time I'd heard him laugh when Carrie wasn't there or the television wasn't on.

"Now, Emmett, you're embarrassing the child," Grandmother said softly as she began cutting another piece of cloth.

I looked back down at my book to hide my face, but I couldn't concentrate on the words in front of my eyes. I was just waiting out the morning until I could go explore a snow-covered Coyote Point.

After lunch was finally over, Grandmother looked as doubtful as she had the first day I'd asked to go into the woods. "The snow's drifted awfully deep," she said.

"Not that deep." Grandfather shoved up from the table. "I'll bet the boy's never seen real snow before."

"It snows in the city," I said.

"And how long is it before the plows and salt trucks are out turning it into something black and dirty?"

"They usually work on the roads all the time it's snowing," I admitted.

"Nobody will have worked on the paths in the woods." Grandfather looked through the window at the snow spread clean and unspoiled across the field.

Grandmother followed his gaze. "Do you remember how Rusty loved the snow? How the two of you would go out tracking in the woods or build snow animals? Snow bears were Rusty's favorite."

Grandfather turned to her. "And you'd make snow cream. Chocolate for Russ, vanilla for me."

"Maybe you could get me some snow later, and I could stir up a batch today. The snow looks perfect for it."

For a minute Grandfather hesitated as he looked back out the window. Then as he went on into the living room, he said, "The boy can get it for you."

"Sure," I said. "How much snow do you want?"

"Oh, I don't know." Grandmother looked down at her hands in her lap. "Maybe I shouldn't make any. They say it isn't safe eating snow cream now what with all the pollution in the air."

In the other room, Grandfather was poking up the fire. He raised up and called to me. "Fill the woodbox before you go. It's cold today."

I was carefully placing the last armload on top of the pile in the woodbox when Grandfather came out on the back porch.

He picked up a piece of wood for the stove and was back to the door before he said, "The snow makes it hard for the animals at the Point, but you can't be bringing in any more to the house, no matter what. Do you understand that, boy?"

"Why, Grandfather? If they're hurt and you can help them, why don't you want to?"

"It's not that easy. Nothing ever is as easy as it sounds." Grandfather lowered the piece of wood to the floor. "Nature's come up with a pretty good plan for survival in the wild, but man's always messing things up. Even when we think we're helping, we mess things up. So it's better to just keep hands off."

"But Grandmother said you used to bring in hurt animals all the time."

"I had to learn my lesson the hard way."

"How?"

When he frowned, I thought he was going to ignore my question, but then he said, "A coyote I brought in once. Smartest animal I'd ever been around. I wasn't sure he didn't know what I was saying."

"What was wrong with him?" I asked when Grandfather fell silent.

"I was never sure. It was a hard year. He might have been starving, but he'd have died if I hadn't brought him in and nursed him. After a while I turned him loose again in the woods."

"Then you did good."

Grandfather's eyes hardened. "Nope. It'd been better to let him die of starvation nature's way than what happened to him. The next year a neighbor caught him in a trap and sold his fur for women's coats." Grandfather balled his fist up and banged it against the wall. "Coat collars."

I was almost afraid to say anything. Yet I wanted to know about the coyotes, so as soon as some of the anger drained away from Grandfather's face, I asked, "Is that what happened to the coyotes around here? People trapped them?"

For a second I thought Grandfather was going to get angry again. Then his shoulders drooped a little as he said, "Only one of the things. They poisoned them and shot them. The state even paid a bounty for their ears and tails."

"Because they killed sheep?"

"That's what the coyote haters said."

I dared one more question. "What would happen if the coyotes came back around here?"

"They'd kill them again," Grandfather said sadly.

It was on the tip of my tongue to tell him about the coyote I'd seen at the Point, but before I could get the words out, he picked up the chunk of wood and went back to the living room.

I listened to him shove the log in the stove before I went back outside. Although I'd shoveled a path from the house to the woodshed, the rest of the snow was unmarked, and I set out across unchartered land.

By the time I got to the woods, my legs already felt weak from pushing through the drifts. Still Grandfather was right. I'd never seen snow before like it was here in the woods. It covered everything, smoothing out the rocks and paths, hanging heavily on the cedar limbs, and even muffling the sounds.

I wished I could somehow walk without touching the snow so that my tracks wouldn't spoil its sparkling beauty. Almost in answer to my wish a wind sprang up and began whipping across my path, wiping out my trail.

At Coyote Point the snow lapped over the edge of the cliff as though it had drifted a few inches too far and now hung there frozen in the air. Down at the bottom, the boulders looked like sleeping giants under their thick covers of white. The creek hadn't iced over and gurgled softly between the snow on each side.

Since it was still early in the afternoon, I decided to walk the creek to the river.

A little way down the creek, I stopped to look back at the cliff towering above me. I had to shade my eyes from the sunshine bouncing off the white limestone rock, the icicles, and the snow while the cave at the bottom was a dark slash of shadow. Chills ran down my spine.

It looked every bit as wild and dangerous as Mom had said, and I wondered for a minute what would happen if I fell there along the creek and broke my leg. How many hours would it take rescuers to find me? Yet I had no doubt they would find me.

I stared at the silent face of the cliff. It knew answers to questions I didn't know to ask. Down through the years other people had stood just as I was standing and stared back at the cliff. My grandfather had, and so had my father.

It didn't matter if I'd never been to the Point with my father or grandfather when snow lay heavy on the ground. I knew at some time in the past they had stood in this very place staring back at the snow-covered cliff for the first time, and now so was I.

After a long time, I turned my back on the cliff and moved on. The water rushing over the rocks in the creek bed and the groan of a tree as it bent to the wind only deepened the natural silence of the place.

Then suddenly I caught another sound faint on the wind. I held my breath while I listened, but there was nothing now. Perhaps the wind through the bare tree limbs had made the whining noise. Breathing again, I stepped carefully from one icy rock to the next on down the creek.

I was out of sight of the cliff when I came to a large pool in the creek. High banks protected it from the wind, and all kinds of tracks marked the snow at its edges. I imagined deer, raccoons, and foxes slipping silently down the hill out of the trees and bushes to the water, each warily watching for enemies. Perhaps they were watching me now.

Although I could see nothing as I let my eyes slide around the area, I felt eyes watching me. Dropping to the ground, I tried to become part of the scenery, but the icy wind hitting my face convinced me in only a few minutes that I'd freeze if I didn't keep moving.

Farther down, the creek was joined by another creek which branched out into a broader valley. The shallow pools of water in this creek were frozen over, but the thin ice cracked under my weight.

Here a new flurry of tracks spilled across the snow, and while they might have been dog tracks, I knew they had to be the coyote's. Bending down, I studied the tracks as they crisscrossed through the snow. There had been more than one animal, and it looked like they'd been making leaps and jumps and tumbles in the snow. They'd played there where the creeks joined, and not too long ago for the wind hadn't wiped away the tracks yet.

I stared up the smaller creek, tempted to follow the trail of the coyotes, but I'd promised myself to walk to the river. Besides, I'd never see the coyote if he didn't want me to see him anyway.

As I began to move away from the tracks, there was the slightest whisper of a noise behind me. Then the coyote brushed past me to stop a few feet beyond. Again I noticed the red surrounding his ears that now were laid back on his head. His muzzle was reddish as well, and I wondered if I gave him the name Red if that would be making him too much of a pet.

His yellow eyes stared into me. Then with his tail tucked low behind him he raised his lips and showed his teeth. Even though the coyote wasn't growling, I fell back a few steps before I realized the animal wasn't threatening me by baring his teeth. Rather he was greeting me in some way.

Slowly I squatted down so that I wouldn't tower so high above him. With his mouth closed now, he kept his eyes on me, his bushy tail tucked low and his ears still back.

He looked away from me up the other valley, his ears lifting as he listened to some sound I couldn't hear. Then he trotted past me back up the creek.

I turned to watch him, but I didn't stand up. Twice he stopped to look back at me, the last time showing his teeth in the strange grin once more.

When he reached the spot where the creeks came together, he halted again. Another few steps and he would be out of sight. Instead of taking them he came charging back to where I still sat motionless. He slid to a sudden stop an arm's reach away from me and made a low sound in his throat.

"Do you want to be friends?" My voice broke through the cold air like ice cracking.

The coyote jumped back, but he didn't run in spite of the panic in his eyes. A panic that seemed to grow as he looked behind him again and then back at me.

He took off up the creek again, but this time just before he would have disappeared from sight he stopped and raised his head to let out a short howl.

The sound that answered him came so quickly I wasn't sure whether it was another coyote or an echo.

I stood up and began slowly walking toward

the coyote, not sure what he'd do next. When I was only a few feet away, he started up the adjoining creek. Every few seconds, he seemed to be checking to see if I was still following.

Then I heard the same sound that I'd caught on the wind earlier, and the coyote raced ahead of me out of sight. I ran as fast as my heavy clothes and boots would let me.

A fallen tree blocked my path up the creek, and I thought the coyote would be long gone by the time I fought my way through the branches. But he was waiting for me on the other side.

Once I was clear of the tree he raced over a slight rise next to the creek. He joined another coyote who was waiting there for him, and when the red-eared coyote began to lick the other one around the mouth, I guessed she must be his mate. As I watched he took her bottom jaw in his mouth and stood there for a minute, not biting, just holding.

The other coyote was smaller than the one who had led me here, with more tracings of black on her back and with a heavy touch of gray on her muzzle. She was lying down, and it wasn't until she began struggling to her feet that I noticed the black iron trap half covered with snow.

Some of the beauty of the place faded as I stared at the iron jaws of the trap biting into the coyote's foot and the spots of red staining the snow.

The red-eared coyote shook his mate's muzzle a little and then moved out from between us.

Panicked fear flowed from the little coyote held in the trap, and she growled fiercely at me.

I thought of Grandfather and wished he was there to tell me what to do. He had warned me not to interfere with nature's way, but this wasn't nature. This was man's doing. Grandfather would help. I looked back toward the cliff, but it was out of sight and the farmhouse a long way beyond that.

By the time I went home and came back, it might be too late for the coyote. Whoever had put out the trap would come back to check it. At the thought I glanced over my shoulder. What if he came now while I hesitated? The trapper wouldn't let me free the coyote.

As I moved a few steps closer to the coyote, she inched away from me as far as the trap would allow her to move. Then she growled even more fiercely.

I stopped in my tracks. She'd tear me apart if I tried to set her free, but I couldn't just leave her to die. I remembered Grandfather's face as he'd said "Coat collars," and my heart began to thud heavily inside my chest.

I had to do something. I looked around at the other coyote, who had jumped up on a rock as though keeping watch.

CHAPTER 7

"I can't help her if she won't let me," I said softly. The words were as out of place there in the wind and the snow as the trap was.

My heart jumped up in my throat as the red-eared coyote hurtled off the rock toward me, but he passed me to land with a savage growl on top of the other coyote. In spite of her trapped leg, the little coyote tried to roll over on her back. The red-eared coyote stood over her for a long moment before he stepped carefully away and looked at me.

Swallowing hard, I moved toward the trap without the hesitation I felt. As I squatted down by the little coyote, I began to make the low crooning noise Grandfather had made while he was working on the rabbit.

The coyote stayed still as I fumbled to find a way to release and pry open the trap. When at last I had freed her foot, she didn't move away, only stared at me. I had to pull the trap away from her.

After I laid the trap aside, I gently took the coyote's foot in my hand. She didn't jerk away. I kept up the crooning noise as I examined the leg to see how much damage had been done. The skin was torn and mangled, but no bones seemed to be broken.

When I let go of her foot and backed away, the other coyote came down off the rock again. This time he approached slowly and licked her muzzle.

Blood stained the snow as she moved away with him. There was none of the playing now, none of the jumping and pouncing in the snow that their earlier tracks had hinted at. She limped away slowly while her mate walked beside her, touching her encouragingly with his nose every few steps. The wind began smoothing away their tracks before they were out of sight.

My eyes fell on the trap. Yanking it out of its anchor in the ground, I pounded it against a rock until it would never again snap on an animal's foot or leg. Then with a yell that echoed through the valley, I slung it as far away as I could. As the sound of my yell died away, the coyote howled up on the hillside behind me.

Back at the farm, I thought I glimpsed Grandmother watching for me at the window as I came back across the field. Then after I did the chores, she fussed over me, made me change into dry clothes, and handed me a cup of steaming hot chocolate when I came downstairs even though supper was bubbling on the stove.

As she herded me into the living room, she said, "You shouldn't stay out so long when it's this cold, Ance. You'll get frostbite."

"I didn't get cold."

"That's the same thing Russell used to say. He'd swear he wasn't cold when he was half frozen just like you are. Something about that place over there makes a Sanford lose his good sense," she grumbled.

"Don't worry about me, Grandmother. I'm all right."

"You might as well tell her to stop breathing," Grandfather said without looking up.

Still muttering under her breath, Grandmother went back to the kitchen. I started to follow her, but Grandfather stopped me. "Leave her be, boy. If she wasn't worrying over you, she'd be worrying over me."

I settled back in the chair, glad of the warmth of the fire and the hot chocolate. I wondered where the coyotes were.

After a while Grandfather said, "Well, boy, how'd it look?"

I jumped, almost spilling my hot chocolate, and wondered how he knew about the coyotes. "What?"

"The snow," Grandfather said.

I remembered the smooth stretches of white with the shifting drifts and how when I'd come back through the woods there'd no longer been any trace of my earlier footprints. "You were right, Grandfather. I'd never seen snow before."

Grandfather nodded and stared at the stove.

"Ruth won't let me go over there in the snow anymore. I guess she's afraid I won't come back." He was quiet for a moment before he added, "Maybe I wouldn't."

The room grew too quiet then, so I began to talk about how the trees had looked with the snow weighing down their branches and how each gust of wind had showered more snow through the air. When I got carried away and told him about the boulders looking like sleeping giants under the snow, I expected him to laugh at me, but he didn't.

Then with the memory of the trap, some of the beauty of the snow faded. "Grandfather," I said. "Did you ever do any trapping?"

Grandfather looked up sharply. "You wanting to trap?"

I shivered, feeling a little sick. "No."

Grandfather looked back down. "When I was your age, I used to have to run my father's trap line every day."

"Trap line?"

"Don't you know anything about trapping?"

"Nobody traps in the city," I said.

Grandfather stared out the window into the dark beyond. "A trapper puts out traps in a line up a creek or somewhere he thinks looks like a rich area. Then every day he has to run his line to get the animals out of the traps."

"Are they dead when he finds them?"

Grandfather looked back at me. "The trapper kills them."

"And you did that?"

"I did. I learned to make my first hit hard and true."

I remembered the coyote in the trap watching me with her yellow eyes. I thought about having to kill her instead of letting her loose, and I met Grandfather's eyes and said, "I'm sorry."

Grandfather nodded a little as he turned his eyes back to the stove. "Well, there were a lot of animals and Pa made good money on his furs. Money we needed."

"And people still run trap lines?"

"Some do."

"I found a trap."

"Where?" Grandfather's head jerked up. "At Coyote Point?"

"Down the creek a way and up a smaller creek."

"How far up?"

"I'm not sure."

"It could be that you got off our land then. We don't own all that creek. Joe Kenton wouldn't sell it to me."

"Joe Kenton? Carrie's father?"

"That's right." Grandfather's eyes narrowed. "He said I was the one who should be selling to him, that he'd give me a good price for the Point, that there wasn't any sense in an old man like me hanging on to it and letting it go wild when he could make something out of it."

"That's crazy."

"I told him as much."

"You think I might have been on his land then?"

"Could be. Did you cross a fence? There used to be some kind of a line fence across the creek."

"I didn't see any." I tried to remember a fence, but I had been intent on following the coyote. "Does Carrie's father trap?"

"The only time I've ever known him to was when they were killing out the coyotes around here years ago, but could be he lets somebody else run a line on his place." Grandfather looked over at me. "How did you come to find the trap?"

"I just came upon it," I said, not sure what Grandfather would think about me setting the coyote free.

"Must not have been hid very good." Grandfather snorted. "Did you leave it alone?"

I hesitated, but I'd already told one half truth. So I said, "I bashed it on the rocks and threw it as far up in the trees as I could."

Grandfather dropped his chin down on his chest, and it was a minute before I realized he was laughing.

"You're not mad?"

"You ought not to do it again," Grandfather said. "Next time you pay attention to the fences, and if you come upon a trap at Coyote Point, just bring it on home. Nobody's got permission to trap on Sanford land."

From the kitchen I heard the sound of Grandmother getting plates and glasses out of the cabinet, and I knew she'd call us to supper soon. So even though Grandfather had turned away from me and shut his eyes, which meant he didn't want to talk anymore, I said, "Did you ever set free any of the animals caught in your father's traps?"

Grandfather didn't open his eyes. "I did. But crippled animals don't stand much chance in the wild. Often as not, I found them dead later on, and I was just taking food out of my family's mouths for nothing."

"Some of them lived though, didn't they?"

"Some, until Pa realized what I was doing. He never forgave me for being so soft."

"The wolf? Was it one of them?"

"It was."

Then to keep me from asking more questions, Grandfather began to noisily stir the fire up.

After supper, I went up to my room, wrapped up in a quilt, and wrote Mom. I reread her letter twice, the second time skipping the part about Dad because those words were burned in my mind already. Still when I picked up my pen, I had a hard time thinking of anything to write.

I told her about school. That took one short paragraph. I wrote about Carrie Ruth and the quilt, which made a little longer paragraph. I tried to describe the way the snow had looked at the Point, but the words didn't come out right. I ended up just telling her that some of the drifts were over the fence posts. I didn't write anything about the coyotes. They were my secret.

Finally by telling her that I was all right and that Grandmother and Grandfather Sanford were all right and saying that I hoped she was all right, I filled up the page and signed my name.

When I read it over, the letter sounded stiff, but I didn't seem to know how to change it. Mom and I had always been able to talk about nearly anything. Over supper she'd tell me about her day, and I'd tell her about mine. But now it was different. Everything was different. The city had become the farm. Our apartment had changed to this old farmhouse that groaned with its age, and the squirrels and birds on campus had given away to a whole woods full of wild animals. But mostly it was different because she had gone away and we had to talk in letters instead of face to face.

A little feather of worry tickled my insides. I couldn't be sure she'd ever come back.

At the bottom of the letter, I added a postscript. "Grandfather says they dragged the river."

Then I folded the letter and sealed it in the envelope. When I wrote Mom's address on the outside, I had to get out the envelope her letter had come in to check the spelling of the town's name.

Before I turned out the light, I looked around the room. The objects in it were more familiar now, but the room wasn't any more mine now than it had been when I first came. All my things were out of sight in the closet or in drawers. I was just borrowing the room for a while.

After I clicked off the lamp, I shut my eyes and opened them again slowly after a moment.

Moonlight bounced off the white ground outside and made it almost light in the room. Just like in the city with the street lamps outside.

I hadn't gotten used to the dark of the country nights. Even though I enjoyed seeing the multitude of stars the true dark of the night revealed, I still didn't like the darkness. A few times when the clouds were thick, I'd been tempted to leave my lamp burning, but I was too old for a night-light.

If Mom had been here I might have been able to tell her about how dark the night sometimes seemed or about how I didn't like looking in the mirror in the bathroom because of the way it bent and changed the way my face looked. Maybe I could tell her why my stereo had to stay in the closet and why I didn't tell Grandmother I wasn't Rusty anymore. But I couldn't write those kinds of things in a letter. I didn't even seem to be able to write to her about the snow on the Point or the coyote in the trap.

I fell to sleep wondering how the little coyote's leg was and if I could have done more for her.

The next day when I went out to put the letter in the mailbox at the end of our lane, the wind had calmed and was no longer shifting the snowdrifts. Cars had left two tracks along the road, but there was ice underneath. School had been canceled again.

I was headed back up the lane, planning how I might track down the coyotes at the Point, when a horn honked out on the road. Carrie was climbing out of her mother's car. With a wave she ran to catch up with me.

"Don't you just love the snow?" she said.

Her cheeks were pink and her brown eyes sparkling. She was probably the prettiest girl I'd ever seen, but all I could think of as I looked at her right then was that Grandmother would think I should stay at the house and visit with Carrie instead of spending most of the day at the Point as I'd planned.

Grandmother and Carrie worked on the quilt all morning while Grandfather napped in his chair. No matter how I tried I couldn't seem to sit still. I'd settle on the couch with a book, but five minutes later I'd be up looking out the window or standing next to the stove.

Finally Grandfather opened his eyes and said crossly, "Why don't you go for a walk, boy?"

Grandmother looked up from the quilt. "He can't do that. It's almost lunchtime, and besides he has company."

"Looks like you're the one who has the company," Grandfather said.

"I'm not company, Aunt Ruth. If Ance wants to do something else, he doesn't have to stay here because of me." Carrie looked up through her lashes at me.

"I haven't got anything else to do," I said.

"Then stop acting like you've got ants in your pants," Grandfather said.

Carrie grinned at me as I sat back down and picked up my book, but I couldn't read. Without realizing what I was doing, I began drumming my fingers on the chair arm.

Grandmother stuck her needle in the quilt and stood up. "Ance, why don't you show Carrie Ruth your room while I put lunch on the table?"

Carrie and I obediently trooped up the stairs. Once in the room she laughed and said, "Do you think Aunt Ruth is trying to play matchmaker?"

I flushed. "She just wants me to have some friends while I'm here, and I guess you're the only likely candidate."

"I doubt that. You could have lots of friends if you wanted to. I'm just the only one Aunt Ruth knows."

"Maybe," I said as I stood in the middle of the floor and watched her.

She looked around and said, "This room looks the same as always. Where's your stuff?"

"I didn't bring much with me."

"Aunt Ruth said you had a stereo."

"It's in the closet."

"The closet?" Carrie looked puzzled. "Why?"

"It just didn't fit out here with Dad's stuff."

Carrie looked around again. "I'd never really thought about it before, but it is kind of a shrine, isn't it?"

"Yeah, well, since I'm only going to be here for a while, I thought maybe I'd just leave everything like it was. Not disturb anything, you know."

"You've got it all wrong, Ance. You ought to

put your father's things away in the closet and set your things out while you're here."

"Maybe."

She just looked at me a minute before she said, "Let's go down and help Aunt Ruth with lunch."

We were both relieved to leave the room behind. After we ate, we went outside and built a snowman to make Grandmother happy. Then Carrie wanted to go for a walk.

"Will you take me to the Point? Uncle Emmett says that's where you go every afternoon."

So I did get to the Point, but I didn't climb down the cliff to search for the coyotes. That would have to wait. There wouldn't have been anything I could have done for the little coyote's wounded foot anyway.

But it was fun taking Carrie through the woods, pointing out the rabbit and bird tracks to her, shaking down a cedar limb of snow on her head, and listening to her laugh.

"I've been over here with Uncle Emmett," she said. "But not for a long time, and never in the snow. It's different in the snow."

"I think maybe it's different every day."

We were standing on the Point, and even as we talked I searched the snow-covered hillsides below us for a brush of yellow and gray fur. If they were there, I couldn't see them.

Carrie's eyes were on me. "It makes Uncle Emmett happy that you like it over here."

"I didn't think anything I did made Grandfather happy."

"He's just tired of being sick right now," Carrie said as we turned and started back for home. "He's really as glad as Aunt Ruth that you're here for the year."

I didn't argue with her even though I didn't think she knew what she was talking about. I just pointed out the red-tailed hawk that was circling high in the air over us.

The night after Carrie had gone home, I went to the barn to do the chores. On top of the feed bin was a can of wound spray for animals. It had never been there before.

I read the label and then looked toward the house—Grandfather knew I'd let an animal out of the trap.

CHAPTER 8

The next day when the sun warmed and the snow began to drip off the eaves, Grandmother let me go without a word.

The tracks Carrie and I had made the day before were still there, a gash in the snow. With the can of wound spray bumping against my side as I walked, I hoped the coyotes' trail would be as easy to find.

I barely paused at the top of Coyote Point before going on down the creek. When I had gone a little way up the second creek, I found the fence, or what was left of it. The wire lay on the ground with snow drifted over it, but it meant that the trap hadn't been on Grandfather's land.

I began watching for tracks as soon as I climbed past the fallen tree. Although I saw no sign of the coyotes, I hadn't gone far when I came upon the prints of a man's boots in the snow.

At the spot where the little coyote had been caught in the trap, the tracks circled around twice, three times, maybe more, as he must have been searching for his trap. My eyes went to the smooth, untouched snow on the hillside where I'd thrown the trap, and I smiled.

It was easy to follow the man's trail straight to his next trap. There were two of them together, baited and ready. When I dropped a rock on the spring trigger of the traps, the iron jaws bit at the air. I wanted to smash these traps as I had the one that had caught the coyote, but I thought maybe I shouldn't. So I left it lying and searched out two more traps, springing them, too.

When I looked around and realized how far I'd come up the creek, I didn't dare go any farther for fear I might come upon the man himself. I cut away from the creek up the hill and then looked back. The sight of my tracks in the snow alongside the trapper's made me a little uneasy. What would the trapper do if he caught me springing his traps?

The thought made me climb the hill away from the creek a little faster, but I kept watching for tracks as I climbed. I was back on Grandfather's land before I stumbled across the trail of a lone coyote.

I had to grab hold of trees and bushes to pull myself along as I followed the tracks along the steep hillside, but the coyote had no such problems. He had moved neatly across the face of the hill without a slip.

When the hill became even steeper, I had to give up on trailing the coyote and just try to find a way up to the top. I began climbing up the rocky bed of a watershed creek. It was easier going, but then, near the top, I slipped on an icy rock and banged my leg as I fell. Sitting up, I gingerly felt the knot rising on my shin.

Coyote Point was a hard place, my mother had warned in her letter. And it was. Rocks and earth and plants and animals. I was simply another of the animals along with the coyotes, foxes, and rabbits. If I climbed slippery rocks up a cliff side, I had to expect bruises. But exploring and finding out more about the Point was worth a few bruises.

Out of the wind and with the sun on my face, I settled more comfortably in the hollowed-out wet-weather creek. If I couldn't find the coyotes that didn't mean I couldn't watch the other animals.

Dark gray snowbirds flew down to peck at the weed tops above the snow, and then all in a rush they'd flutter back up to the tree branches even though I made no sound or movement and heard none. A few minutes later they'd be on the ground again, but always ready for flight.

Again the birds took wing suddenly, but this time they didn't settle back on the ground after a few moments but stayed in the trees. Moving my head slowly, I looked around to see why.

To my right, the red-eared coyote was standing motionless beside a bushy little cedar. "Where's the little one?" I asked softly as I rose slowly to my feet.

The coyote also moved slowly as he stepped

away from the cover of the tree toward me. Then all at once he whirled and trotted away. I followed him through the low-hanging tree limbs, almost losing him twice, but just when I was about to give up and turn back, he'd be there in front of me again.

The little coyote was waiting for him in a protected hollow deep in the woods. She whined when she saw him and began limping painfully toward him until she caught my scent on the air and stopped.

The red-eared coyote bolted over to her and shoved her neck with his nose as if to make her pay attention to him instead of me. She looked toward me one more time, but then as if she trusted him completely, she ignored me and began licking his muzzle in greeting.

He heaved and deposited the contents of his stomach at her feet. She ate greedily while he moved out of the hollow to higher ground. When she was finished, she turned her back on me and curled up in the sun.

I started to leave, to just slip away through the trees, but the wound spray was burning in my pocket. As quietly as I could I eased around in front of her. She raised her head with her ears pointed forward and fixed her eyes on me. Then she glanced to where the red-eared coyote still kept watch, and he lifted his voice in a series of yips and yowls. She joined in on the last howl before she looked back at me.

"It's all right, little one," I said in a singsong

tone. "I'm just going to look at your foot again. It's all right. You don't have to be afraid."

Pulling off my gloves, I kept up the soft crooning as I took the can out of my pocket. Quickly I sprayed the medicine on the coyote's foot, but at the hissing sound the little coyote jerked back with a snarl. The red-eared coyote bounded over to join her.

I sat very still while I kept up the soft crooning words. The growl died in the little coyote's throat as she slid around behind her mate. For some reason, I felt no fear as I stared into the bigger coyote's eyes.

He stepped closer to me, his ears back and his teeth bared. I smiled too and held out my hand.

Before I knew what was happening he grabbed my hand in his mouth. He didn't bite down but just held my hand for a long moment until the little coyote got jealous and pushed her head under his neck. Then he carefully removed his mouth. A soft impression of his teeth traced the back of my hand.

The coyotes turned and began making their way slowly out of the hollow and through the trees. They hadn't gone far when the red-eared coyote stopped and looked back at where I still sat in the hollow. He lifted his nose and howled once. The sound seemed to be a promise.

The Point seemed friendlier as I walked home. Even the hawk's high-pitched whistle sounded almost like a greeting to me from high above.

The sun had melted enough of the snow that the tracks I'd made on the way over to the Point were melting into puddles now. With a relieved smile, I thought of how my tracks along the trap line would be melting, too.

After that I went to Coyote Point every day and searched out the trapper's line. Day by day I grew bolder until I was springing as many as six traps. He placed them in different locations and hid them well, but I still found them even after the snow melted and there were no tracks to guide me. I set free two foxes and a big possum, spraying the antiseptic on their wounded legs before I released them from the spell of the crooning noise I made.

I didn't try to find them the next day. Nor did I search out the little coyote again. I'd done all I could do for her, and there was no need frightening her more just to satisfy my need to know that she was okay.

So I didn't see her, but I did see the red-eared coyote. He came often to the crest of the hill to watch me as I walked along the creek. Sometimes he'd follow me by walking along the top of the hill, keeping me in sight far below.

I began to feel better than I had since Mom had driven away New Year's Eve. The year wasn't going to be as bad as I'd expected. I was growing fond of Grandmother and Grandfather, and through them I was getting to know my dad as I never had. While his disappearance was still as much of a mystery as always, I was learning other things about him and at the same time about myself.

I had learned where to stand in the bathroom

to make my features look normal in the mirror over the sink, and while my stereo was still in the closet, I did sometimes bring a rock back from the Point to add to my father's collection.

I didn't tell anybody about the coyotes. Not even Mom in my letters although I still had to search for words to fill the page. I was tempted more than once to tell Carrie, but I kept remembering that it might be her father who had the trap line.

Then one day when I came back across the field from the Point, a black truck was pulled up to the house. Grandfather, with no hat or coat on, stood on the porch talking to a man beside the truck.

Even before I got near enough to hear the other man's words or voice, I could tell he was angry. He kept pointing toward the woods and gesturing.

"Ask the boy," Grandfather said when he saw me coming up behind the man.

"I don't need to do any asking. I already know," the man said with a glance over his shoulder at me. "I'm here to do some telling."

Grandfather's face stayed stone calm. "You've already said what you think more than once, but you don't know anything for sure till you ask him."

"Ask me what?" I moved up beside Grandfather on the porch.

Grandfather turned his eyes from the man to me. "This is Joe Kenton."

"Carrie's dad?"

"That's right," Mr. Kenton said. His eyes narrowed as he looked me over.

I wanted to get away from his accusing stare by slipping inside past Carrie and Grandmother, who were standing in the door. He knew what I'd been doing. Instead I made myself stand still on the porch and meet his eyes. I'd known I'd have to pay for springing the traps from the very first day I'd followed the trapper's footprints in the snow, and while I wasn't sorry I'd sprung the traps, I was sorry the trapper had turned out to be Carrie's father.

"What were you doing anyway, kid? Playing some kind of game?" Mr. Kenton's face turned a shade redder as I just shook my head a little.

Behind us Carrie pulled away from Grandmother and came out the door onto the porch. "Now don't get so upset, Daddy."

"This hasn't got anything to do with you, Carrie," he said.

Carrie looked down and let Grandmother pull her back inside. Before Grandmother closed the door, I could see her worried eyes on Grandfather.

But Grandfather seemed calm enough as he turned to me and said, "Mr. Kenton claims you've been running his trap line stealing his furs. Have you?"

I swallowed hard as I looked first at Joe Kenton, then back at Grandfather. "I didn't steal any furs. I just sprang the traps."

"I told you, Emmett," Mr. Kenton said. "And you know that's the same as stealing."

Grandfather kept his eyes on me. "Did you release any animals from the traps?"

I nodded. "Two foxes and a possum."

Grandfather turned back to Kenton. "How many other furs do you think he may have cost you?"

"I'm not trapping for furs. I'm running the traps to catch those coyotes I've been hearing."

"Coyotes?"

"Don't let on like you haven't heard them, Emmett. They're back in these parts again, and you're just lucky you don't have any sheep for them to kill."

"They bothering your sheep?" Grandfather asked.

"I aim to be rid of them before that happens."

"Coyotes are sometimes hard to trap."

"Especially when somebody keeps springing your traps." Joe Kenton looked at Grandfather. "It wouldn't surprise me if you put him up to it."

Grandfather just stared back at him, and after a minute Kenton lowered his eyes and muttered, "I mean I know you wouldn't do that, but you've always been soft on animals."

"Get my billfold off the mantle, boy," Grandfather said to me.

I scooted past Grandmother and Carrie in the hallway, not looking at either of them. I had the feeling Carrie was trying just as hard not to look at me. When I handed Grandfather his wallet, he opened it and pulled out several bills. "Here. This should pay your losses."

"I don't want your money, Emmett. You know that."

The money fluttered in the wind as Grandfather kept it held out toward him. "What do you want, Joe?"

"You just keep the boy away from my traps."

"He won't bother your traps again," Grandfather said.

Mr. Kenton looked over at me. "And stay off my land."

I met his eyes. "I will."

"I guess that'll have to be good enough." He looked at the door. "Come on, Carrie Ruth. We've got to get home."

As Carrie came out the door carrying her coat, I searched for something to say to her, but she kept her eyes on the ground.

After she got in the truck Grandfather folded the money back into his wallet. He looked up at Joe Kenton and said, "The boy's given you his word. Now you give me yours that you'll stay off my land with your traps and your guns."

"If those coyotes get into my sheep, I'll track them down and shoot them wherever they are."

"Not on Coyote Point."

"A man has to be half crazy to like coyotes, Emmett."

Grandfather just stared at him, and Carrie's father looked away first. Without another word he climbed into the truck, spun it around, and threw up a few rocks as he took off down the lane.

When the truck was out of sight, Grandfather

slumped a little, and a shiver ran through him. Opening the door, Grandmother said, "Come inside before you catch your death of cold."

As we went inside she kept up a steady stream of fussing. "If you were going to stand outside all day you should have put on your hat and coat. Whoever heard the like." She glanced over at me. "Stir up the fire, Ance, while I fix your grandfather something warm to drink."

Grandfather sank down into his chair. His hands trembled on the chair arms, but when he saw me looking at them, he grasped the arms tightly to stop their shaking. I turned away to poke the fire, realizing just how weak Grandfather was.

"I'm sorry, Grandfather," I said after I'd pushed a fresh chunk of wood into the fire and it was roaring with a burst of heat.

Grandfather leaned back his head and shut his eyes as he rocked a little. "I figured you were up to something like this." He opened his eyes and looked at me. "Did the coyote you set free live?"

My eyes widened. "I didn't say anything about setting a coyote free."

"You didn't have to. I saw it in your eyes when Joe was talking about tracking down the coyotes." Grandfather leaned back again. "One thing you don't have to worry about. That coyote won't get caught in the trap again. You can't trick a coyote but once."

"But he still might shoot them."

"He might."

I moved away from the fire over to the window. After a while I said, "He was awful mad. Do you think he'll make Carrie stop coming over here?"

"I don't know," Grandfather said.

Grandmother came back in the living room in time to hear my last question. "No, of course not. Carrie Ruth has to keep coming. We haven't finished the quilt." She handed Grandfather the cup of hot cider and tucked a blanket around his legs while she talked. "As long as you stay off his land, Ance, everything will be all right."

"You'll have to do that, Little Russ," Grandfather said. "A Sanford always keeps his word."

My eyes flew to Grandfather. That was the first time he'd called me anything but "boy" since I came. Little Russ. For a minute I thought he, like Grandmother with her Rusty, had slipped back in time, but then I remembered. Before my father had disappeared, Grandfather had always called me Little Russ.

CHAPTER 9

A whole week went by without Carrie climbing down off the bus with me at the farm. I wanted to talk to her, but every time I was close to her she'd be busy talking to someone else. After a while I quit trying to get her attention. On the bus I went to the back and stared out the window at the fields and houses until I got to school or to the farm.

At the house nobody mentioned Carrie, but every day when I came in from the bus, Grandmother and Grandfather would look up eagerly. Then when I was always alone, their faces would fall. Gloom settled over the house.

Grandfather had caught a cold, and he huddled in his chair by the fire hardly saying a word for hours on end. Grandmother fussed over him and worked on her quilt pieces. Neither of them mentioned Carrie Ruth although Grandmother often looked longingly at the quilt frames pushed back against the wall.

On Thursday Carrie's favorite brownies were

on the table when I came in from school. I didn't have much appetite for them, but I forced down a couple before I took off for the woods.

That night Grandfather's cough was worse. On a trip to the kitchen for a drink of water, he bumped into the quilting frames. "Why don't you finish this thing and get it out of the middle of the floor?" he said crossly.

Without a word, Grandmother set down her basket of new quilt pieces and moved her chair over to the quilting frames.

In my regular spot on the couch, I tried to read my history assignment, but I couldn't concentrate. It was my fault that Carrie was staying away. It would have been better for them if I had been the one to stay away. I'd brought them nothing but trouble and bad memories.

The heavy ticking of the old clock and Grandfather's cough were loud in the silence of the room. The television was off because it hurt Grandfather's eyes. When Grandfather wasn't coughing, I could hear the pull of Grandmother's needle and thread through the quilt.

I wanted to tell them I was sorry I'd caused Carrie to stay away, but it seemed silly to just look up and say "I'm sorry."

I was glad when the clock chiming nine times meant I could escape up the steps to a different kind of quiet. At least the silence in my father's old bedroom couldn't be my fault.

Upstairs, I opened the closet, plugged the stereo into the nearest outlet, and turned the radio on with the volume barely turned up. I lay down on the floor with my ear close to the speaker and read Mom's last letter again.

She'd made her first find, and she wrote practically a whole page about the shards of a bowl she'd found. Following that were the usual questions about school and Grandmother and Grandfather plus one about Carrie and the quilt. I skimmed over that part to get to the last page.

> It's only natural for you to be curious about your father, Ance [she wrote]. You're at an age when a father becomes especially important to a boy. That's one reason I thought it would be such a good idea for you to stay with your grandparents this year. Your grandfather and your father were so close that I suppose I hoped you'd work out the same sort of relationship with him. Grandfather Sanford always had so much patience with you when you were little, but I guess the years can change people. Still I have a hard time believing he doesn't like you. Maybe you're not trying hard enough to like him.

The song on the radio seemed to get louder, and I turned the volume even lower. Then I stared at the red lights on the control panel a few minute before I started reading again.

> And I understand your need to know what happened to your father. I'm sorry I'm not

there to talk it out with you. I guess the next best thing is for you to write down all your questions and send them to me. I don't have all the answers, but I do know this. Your father loved us. So as crazy as your grandmother's idea of amnesia may seem, it would be nearer the truth than your grandfather's idea that Russell walked away and left us. I've never understood how Father Sanford could believe that.

I folded her letter and put it back in the envelope. Then with my eyes shut, I listened to the music coming out of the speaker. I didn't want to think. But the song ended and a commercial came on. I couldn't keep the thoughts away.

Sitting up, I leaned back against the closet door and stared down at the envelope with the strange stamps and Mom's familiar handwriting. She was trying to help, but I didn't know what questions to ask.

Down in the room below me I could hear Grandmother and Grandfather getting ready for bed. I didn't have to look at my clock to know it was a quarter till ten. They had a routine and a time for everything. Mom had warned me about that before I'd come to the farm, but she hadn't warned me about how I might mess up that routine.

From below I could hear Grandfather coughing, and something squeezed tight in my own chest.

The next morning when I got on the bus, I went straight to Carrie's seat. Without any kind of greeting, I said, "Why haven't you been to the house?"

She looked down at her books. "You know why," she said softly.

"Is it because your father won't let you?" When she didn't answer, I went on. "Because of me?"

"You shouldn't have bothered his traps, Ance."

"Have you ever seen an animal caught in one of those things?" I stared straight ahead at the bus driver's head. "It's awful."

"Animals are just animals. They don't feel things like people do."

"How can you be sure of that?" I shook myself a little. "But that doesn't matter now. I told your father I wouldn't bother his traps anymore. I haven't and I won't."

She was still staring at her books, and I thought how odd it was to be talking to Carrie without hearing her laugh and seeing her smile. I took a deep breath and plunged on. "Grandmother and Grandfather miss you."

"I know, but I thought I'd just wait till things calmed down a little before I came back."

"Grandfather made Grandmother start working on the quilt again last night. He's got this awful cough, and he's crosser even than usual."

"He'll get to feeling better."

"Yeah, probably, but you coming back to see

them would make them both feel better faster."

"They don't need me now. They have you."

"I'm just a problem for them," I said with a sigh. "But anyway, if I'm the reason your father won't let you come, I promise to stay away while you're at the house. I'll stay at the barn or something."

"I didn't say Daddy wouldn't let me come." Carrie looked up with a smile then for the first time since I'd sat down beside her. "Besides, you were always off in the woods every time I came anyway."

"I was there part of the time."

"Until you could escape to the Point. What do you do over there?"

"You mean besides springing your father's traps?"

She couldn't keep from laughing then, but after her laugh faded away she said solemnly, "I'm sorry, Ance, but when Daddy gets mad, there's no talking to him."

"I guess he had a right to yell at me, but I got the feeling that it wasn't just the traps. The way he kept looking at me made me feel funny. What did he say after you left?"

"Oh, I don't know. Something about how he never knew a Sanford who wasn't a little strange and that if you were letting animals out of his traps that had to mean you were even stranger than most." She dropped her eyes. "And a lot of stuff like that."

"What stuff?"

"Nothing important. Daddy doesn't always make sense when he gets mad. Mama says if I wait awhile it'll all blow over."

"Yeah, I guess." Again I thought of the gloom that had fallen over the farmhouse. "But they really miss you, and I just thought maybe if it would make a difference, I could disappear while you visited them."

She shook her head. I stood up and went to the back to stare out the window. I'd tried. That was all I could do—try.

That afternoon when Carrie climbed off the bus behind me, I was so happy I couldn't stop grinning.

She grinned back at me. "You look like you just got up on Christmas morning."

"You don't know how glad I am you came. I feel like hugging you."

Her smile changed a little as she looked up at me through her dark lashes. "That might be fun."

I stared down at the ground to hide my face that was suddenly burning hot.

With a laugh she started up the lane for the house. When I didn't follow right away, she turned and said, "Well, come on, Ance. I promise not to bite."

My face was still flaming red and she was still laughing at me, but I didn't care. I was too glad she was there. Then I remembered her father. "Maybe I shouldn't."

"What do you mean?" She shifted her load of books from one arm to the other.

"Your father."

"Oh, don't worry about Daddy," she said and flipped her long hair back over her shoulder.

"Does he know you're here?"

"No, but Mama does. She's going to bring Uncle Emmett something for his cough when she comes to pick me up."

"Maybe it'd be better if I just disappeared like I told you I would."

"I wish you'd quit talking about disappearing." She frowned at me before she started on toward the house. "It might really happen."

"What?" I hurried a few steps to catch up with her.

"You disappearing. You spend so much time over at Coyote Point." She gave me a sidelong glance as she went on. "And that's where your father disappeared."

"I'm not going to really disappear," I said. "I just meant I'd stay away while you were here."

"How do you know you won't disappear? Do you think your father thought he'd disappear?"

"I don't know."

She looked over at me and then at the ground. "I asked my father about it. He and your father didn't get along, but he helped with the search. Everybody in the neighborhood did. He said they covered every inch of ground for miles and they couldn't find a trace. He said it was like the earth had opened up and swallowed your father."

"What does he think happened to my father?" I asked.

With her face turned away from me, Carrie muttered, "I don't know."

"Yes, you do. He thinks Dad deserted us like Grandfather does."

Carrie looked at me. "That doesn't mean it's true."

"It doesn't matter what they think," I said. "I guess all that matters is what I believe."

At the barn when Geraldine came out to meet us, I ran my hand all along the cat's back and listened to the dry crackle of her fur. Carrie had never asked to rub Geraldine any more after that first day.

Now as she waited while I greeted the cat, Carrie asked, "What do you believe?"

"I'm not sure, but I do know Dad didn't just go away and leave us." I looked past the barn to the trees beyond. "Even if he could have deserted Mom and me, I just don't think he could have left the Point and never seen it again."

Carrie shifted her weight of her books from one arm to the other again. "That's a weird thing to say, Ance."

"I guess it is." I gave Geraldine one last stroke before I stood up. "But then, remember? I'm a little strange."

Carrie looked worried. "I'm sorry if I hurt your feelings. But you asked me what Daddy said."

"My feelings aren't hurt." I smiled as I realized it was true. If liking animals made me strange, then I didn't mind being strange.

When she started on for the house, I stayed where I was. After a few steps she looked back. "Aren't you coming?"

"Maybe I'd better just stay out here."

"Oh, Ance. Come on and eat some of Aunt Ruth's brownies. Then you can go hide out at the Point until I've gone home if you want to."

I moved up beside her slowly. "I've probably gotten you into enough trouble already just getting you to come. I don't want to get you in more trouble for talking to me."

"I came because I wanted to, and I'll talk to you if I want to. Daddy doesn't really care if we're friends."

I grinned again like I had when she'd gotten off the school bus with me. "Even if I am a little weird?"

She didn't answer me, but she laughed as she ducked in the back door.

There were no brownies or cookies on the table. Nothing steamed or boiled on the stove, and the kitchen seemed so empty that for a minute I thought no one was home. But then I heard the rumble of Grandfather's coughing.

As I went on into the living room, I felt like I was bringing them a gift. I couldn't wait till they saw Carrie following me.

Grandfather's eyes did light up before another spasm of coughing took hold of him.

"Uncle Emmett, you sound awful," Carrie said.

"I've heard worse," Grandfather said between coughs.

"Where's Grandmother?" I asked.

"She went to lie down awhile."

"Is she sick?"

Grandfather looked at me. "Old people need naps sometimes."

"Oh, Uncle Emmett," Carrie said with a big smile. "You and Aunt Ruth aren't old."

"And grass ain't green," Grandfather said shortly as he leaned up to open the stove to check the progress of the fire. He poked at the embers a minute before he looked at me again. "Don't just stand there, boy. Go tell your grandmother that Carrie Ruth's here."

I hesitated in the bedroom door. The shades were drawn, and the room was dark.

"Grandmother," I said softly as I moved over to the foot of the big bed.

Grandmother's eyes fluttered a little before she opened them and looked at me. "Rusty? Is that you?"

"Carrie Ruth is here to work on the quilt, Grandmother."

She didn't act like she heard me. Instead she smiled and said, "I always knew you'd come back. We have to tell your father."

My heart began beating too fast. I cleared my throat and stepped around to the side of the bed. "You're having a dream, Grandmother. I'm Ance, remember?"

She blinked her eyes several times while the

joy that had flooded her face faded. "Ance, of course. What time is it?"

"I just got in from school. Carrie Ruth came home with me."

"Oh my goodness," Grandmother said as she sat up and felt for her shoes on the floor by the bed. "I didn't aim to sleep so long. And you say Carrie Ruth is here, too?"

When she looked up and saw Carrie standing in the doorway, some of the light came back into her eyes. "Don't you worry, honey, I've still got some of your brownies. I didn't let Ance eat them all."

"You're going to make me fat, Aunt Ruth," Carrie said with laugh. But then when Grandmother went by her through the door, Carrie's eyes came back to me, and all the smile faded. I knew she'd heard Grandmother call me Rusty.

"She just does that sometimes," I said. "It doesn't mean anything."

"No, of course not," she said. Still she looked like she felt so sorry for me that for a second I wanted to smash my hand through the wall.

After she followed Grandmother toward the kitchen, I looked around the dim room while I waited for my heart to slow down. My eyes caught on a high school picture of my father. His hair was cut short and he had a silly grin on his face, the same kind of smile the photographers always seemed to catch on my face.

We looked so much alike it wasn't any wonder that Grandmother called me Rusty when she wasn't thinking. I sat the picture carefully back on the chest. Sometimes I wished I could be Rusty for her.

CHAPTER 10

We ate enough brownies to make Grandmother happy, and then I left Grandmother and Carrie working on the quilt. I was glad to get away from Carrie, whose smile had slipped away every time she looked at me. I'd had a hard time smiling at all, but Grandmother hadn't noticed. She was too glad to have Carrie there.

When I'd asked if it would be all right if I went to Coyote Point, Grandmother hadn't even looked up. After a minute Grandfather had raised his head a little without actually looking at me and said, "Go."

As I moved across the field toward the trees, the afternoon sun was warm on my back. The snow had melted completely away even in the deepest shade. The ground was moist and spongy underfoot, and the air had a fresh, new smell.

Once in the shadow of the trees, I looked back at the open field and enjoyed the feeling that the trees were hiding me, helping me to disappear.

The thought brought me up short and made me remember what Carrie had said. My father had disappeared forever by walking into these woods. I didn't want to disappear like that.

I didn't want to think about that, either. It didn't do any good to think about it, because no matter which trail I followed in my mind, I always ended up at a dead end. I was beginning to think I'd never know what happened to my father.

I couldn't search for clues now, five years later. Besides, if Grandfather had searched the Point for days and even months without finding out what had happened to Dad, how could I expect to? Grandfather knew this place like the back of his hand.

That's the way I wanted to know it. Moving through the trees, I began to tune my senses to the surrounding woods. I didn't know what exactly I expected to see or hear, but whatever it might be, I didn't want to miss it because I wasn't ready.

I didn't spot the red-eared coyote as I made my way along the familiar path to the Point. I was always disappointed when he didn't show up to walk, if not actually with me, then close by, and I kept searching the bushes and trees for some sign of him.

When I moved off the path into the cavelike shadows of a heavy growth of cedars, a whirring of wings made me jump. I scared the bird up again as I pushed under the low-handing cedar branches, but I never spotted it though I tried. The Point had a way of keeping its secrets well.

The coyote hadn't appeared by the time I got to the Point, so I settled down in my favorite spot at the top of the path leading down the cliff. After a few minutes the little mouse scampered out of his crevice in the cliff. He had gotten so used to me sitting in his territory that he hardly glanced in my direction as he passed by me.

"Hello there, Brownie," I said softly. "I guess you like this weather better than the snow."

Ignoring the sound of my voice, the mouse continued his nonstop search for food. A crow cawed, and I turned my eyes away from the mouse to watch two of the blackbirds flap by overhead.

Suddenly, out of nowhere, the red-eared coyote rushed past me to pounce on the mouse.

"Wait," I yelled, but it was too late. The coyote crunched his jaws, and Brownie was gone.

With glittering eyes, the coyote turned to face me. Then he barked once, and I wasn't sure whether it was to claim his territory or to brag about his kill.

"It's not much to brag about," I said. "Poor little Brownie, fooled into forgetting about his enemies because I was here messing up his alarm defenses."

The coyote laid back his ears and showed his teeth in his odd grin almost as if he thought I'd scouted out the meal for him, and now he was thanking me. Unable to resist, I tried to bare my teeth back at him.

The coyote moved past me back up on the hill where he raised his head and let loose a yowling howl. Throwing back my head, I attempted a howl of my own. Even though my howl sounded nothing like his, it seemed to please him. He trotted a few steps closer to me and wagged his bushy tail a bit.

After that the coyote was always waiting when I got to the Point. Sometimes he'd be waiting for me on the rock at the Point. Other times he'd step out of the bushes in front of me down on the creek. Once he even met me at the edge of the woods.

A few times I spotted his friend, the little coyote, shadowing us, but each time she melted back into the bushes at once. I had the feeling she disapproved of the whole thing.

I wanted to tell Grandfather about my walks with the red-eared coyote, but I didn't think he'd approve, either. Still I couldn't see what it would hurt if I walked with the coyote.

But then I'd remember the little brown mouse. No matter how many times I told myself he might have become the coyote's meal even if I hadn't been there, I could never quite convince myself. So I kept quiet about the red-eared coyote.

Still, even though I didn't tell him, I think Grandfather knew I'd made friends with the coyote, the same as he'd known I'd let a coyote out of the trap.

Every night when I came in after doing my chores, he'd ask, "How were things at the Point?"

I began watching for special sights I could share with him, like the hawk rising out of a tree to circle above me or a tree giving in to the pull of gravity to fall down the steep hillside or the sight of the first spring flowers. Nodding, Grandfather would look out the window toward the Point as though he could see it for himself.

I determined that when warm weather came, I'd take him to the Point with me. But now the late afternoons were still cold, and Grandfather hadn't shaken off his cough in spite of the medicine Carrie's mother brought him from the doctor's office where she worked as a nurse.

Carrie didn't come to the farm every day, but she came at least once and sometimes twice a week to work on the quilt. She said her father had calmed down and decided I was harmless.

"Harmless?" I'd said. "I'm not sure I like that."

Carrie had laughed. "Why not? I think it describes you pretty well."

One day Carrie was still there when I came in from Coyote Point. She came out to the woodshed while I was feeding Jake.

The dog's tail whipped against the ground when he saw her. "At least somebody around here likes me," she said as she bent down to pat the old dog.

"Everybody around here likes you." I set

Jake's food down practically under his nose. He could hardly get up anymore.

"Really?" Carrie looked up at me. "Are you sure about that?"

I ducked my head away from her eyes and leaned over to scratch Jake behind the ears. "Well, maybe Geraldine doesn't, but Jake here does."

Carrie looked back at the dog. "He's getting in bad shape, isn't he?"

"Grandfather doesn't think he'll live out the year." I stood up. "It's funny. Old Jake was one of the things I really looked forward to when Mom decided to leave me here for a year. I thought we'd be able to explore the woods together, and I even thought about having a dog of my own. Mom had said I could and that we'd find a way to keep him in the city when she came back. I guess she was feeling guilty about leaving me."

"Why don't you get a pup then?"

"Grandfather says they're too old to fool with a pup." I began picking up an armload of wood. "I think they're too old to fool with me, too."

"What do you mean?" Carrie ran along beside me as I carried my load of wood toward the porch.

I dumped it and went back outside where I stared up at the first evening star a minute before I answered. "I don't know. It's just that I can't make them feel better like you." I looked from the star to Carrie. "You go in and they smile and laugh. I go in and there's gloom."

"Maybe that's because I smile and laugh, too."

"I smile and laugh."

"Yeah, sure you do. At least once a day," Carrie said. "Is that while you're over at the Point?"

"Maybe." I went to the woodshed and began piling wood on my arm. As I carried it back to the porch past Carrie, who was still standing in the same place, I wouldn't look over at her. It didn't help that she was right. I did smile a lot while I was in the woods now that the red-eared coyote dogged my steps.

Carrie reached out to stop me as I went past her to the woodshed again, but I shook off her hand. "I've got to get the wood in before dark."

"I'll help you." Following me to the pile of wood, she began picking up pieces. "I'm sorry if I made you mad, Ance."

"I'm not mad."

"Yes, you are."

"No, I'm not." I turned toward her. "If it wasn't so dark in here, you could see I'm smiling."

"Okay. I shouldn't have said that about you not smiling."

I sighed as I stood up. "Maybe it was true, and maybe I should try harder. I just don't want to cause them any problems."

"They're really glad you came to stay with them," Carrie said as she stood up with her load of wood, too. "I know they are."

We didn't talk any more until we put the last

load in the woodbox. Then as she tried to brush off her coat, I said, "You shouldn't have helped me. You got all dirty."

"It'll wash," she said. "Aren't you going to ask me why I'm still here?"

"I figured your mother was late for some reason."

"Nope. I'm staying for supper. We're having a celebration because we finished the quilt. Aunt Ruth is in the kitchen fixing up something fancy."

"Maybe we should go help her."

"I tried, but she chased me out to talk to you."

"Well, we've talked. What do you want to do now?"

Carrie grinned. "Let's go back outside and look at the stars. Daddy has all these security lights at the house and barn at home, so you can't see the stars like you can here."

Stars were popping out all over the darkening sky. We kept pointing out new ones to each other until suddenly it was fully dark and there were dozens, maybe hundreds, of stars.

"They're beautiful, aren't they?" Carrie said, reaching over to take my hand.

I nodded.

"Why don't you like me?" Carrie asked.

She wasn't looking at the stars anymore. Neither was I. "I do like you," I finally managed to say.

"You do?"

"Of course I do. You're about the prettiest girl I've ever met." Since the night was hiding my flaming face, I didn't have too much trouble adding, "And the nicest."

"But do you think you could ever like me as a, you know, as a girlfriend?"

Just as I was about to get up nerve to answer, the silence of the night was shattered by the sound of howling.

"What was that?" Carrie said. She moved closer to me, and I felt her shiver.

"Dogs maybe," I said even though I knew it was the coyotes. I'd already picked out the sound of the red-eared coyote's howl, and although I'd never seen the little coyote actually howling, I knew the higher yips and yowls were hers. The two seemed to be blending their voices, and as I listened chills ran through me that had nothing to do with the cool evening air.

"It's coyotes," Grandfather said behind us.

Neither of us had heard Grandfather come outside, and we both jumped a little. My face flamed even hotter as I wondered how long he'd been standing behind us.

Carrie must have had the same thought because she pulled her hand away from mine and said, "Uncle Emmett, you scared us."

"If you paid attention to what's around you, you'd have known I was here."

"We were looking at the stars," Carrie said.

"They're up there all right," Grandfather said.

"And you say that's coyotes howling?" Carrie turned back to look in the direction of the woods.

"The boy could have told you that. He's met them."

I could feel Grandfather's eyes on me, and I kept my head ducked even though I knew he wouldn't be able to see my eyes in the dark.

"Have you, Ance?"

"I've seen them," I said reluctantly, edging around the truth.

"Will you take me with you sometimes so that I can see them, too?" Carrie asked. Even in the dark I thought I caught the excited glow of her eyes. "Daddy says they're worse pests than rats, but I think it'd be fun to really see a wild one out in the woods."

"You could go with me, but I couldn't promise you'd see anything. Coyotes are good at hiding when they want to."

"But you saw them," Carrie said.

"Because they let me."

Grandfather cleared his throat. "Ruth sent me out here to get you. Supper's on the table."

Carrie ran on into the house, but I stayed a minute longer listening for the coyotes. Grandfather waited with me. Their howls split through the night again and brought the thrill back to me.

"You shouldn't lie, boy," Grandfather said when the coyotes fell quiet once more.

"I thought maybe she'd tell her father."

"Joe Kenton's got ears. He knows about the coyotes already."

I tried to swallow the lump that jumped up in my throat. "But I'm afraid he'll shoot them."

"It might happen," Grandfather said.

"But I don't want it to."

"Nobody ever wants bad things to happen, but they happen anyway."

I knew he wasn't just talking about the coyotes now, and the night grew darker and colder. Grandfather began coughing, and when I put my hand on his arm, I could feel him shivering.

"Let's go in, Grandfather. Grandmother and Carrie will be waiting for us."

As we went in the door, the coyotes broke into song again.

CHAPTER 11

With spring near, the sun warmed, turning the fields green and swelling the tree buds. The animals at the Point began to shake off winter and come out of their holes and burrows. When I told Grandfather about two skunks who crossed my path without seeming to know I was there, he said, "It's mating season."

Grandmother looked up from her quilt pieces. "Now don't you get too close to those skunks, Ance. They might have rabies."

"The boy knows better than to bother skunks, rabid or not," Grandfather said. "He wouldn't want to get perfumed."

"You did once," Grandmother countered.

Grandfather smiled a little as he looked over at Grandmother. "So maybe the boy's smarter than me."

"What happened, Grandfather?"

"I always did move quiet in the woods, and I come up on the skunk without giving him proper warning." Grandfather chuckled. "Your grandmother made me strip down out in the yard and wash with tomato juice."

"That's the only thing that'll take away the smell," Grandmother said as she laughed, too. I joined in, and it was almost like Carrie was there.

Now that the quilt was finished, Carrie didn't come to the farm as often as she had. She still climbed down off the school bus with me on Thursdays and sometimes her mother brought her over on Sunday afternoons.

On one of those afternoons, I took her to the Point. As we walked along under the trees, a red squirrel followed us through the treetops, chattering companionably. The red-tailed hawk glided in circles above us, and in the distance we could hear the angy squabble of a bunch of crows. A rabbit bounded across our path, and I showed her the tree where the possum, hanging by his tail from one of the branches, slept away the day.

But we didn't see the coyotes. Once I thought I caught sight of a bushy tail slipping behind a bush, but I couldn't be sure.

Carrie was disappointed when I told her I didn't think the coyote was going to come out, but the doe and fawn almost made up for it. We watched the mother and baby move slowly away through the trees. When they had disappeared, Carrie said, "Why aren't the animals afraid of you, Ance?"

"What makes you think they're not?"

"The deer didn't run."

"She didn't stay where she was, either."

"She probably would have if I hadn't been with you."

"Maybe," I said. With the woods full of the sound of birds and Carrie's hand in mine, I felt things were close to perfect.

We sat down in the sunshine in a little clearing in the midst of the trees.

"Uncle Emmett always said it was the Indian in him. That the animals knew he respected them, and that's the reason they weren't afraid of him."

"Has he ever brought you to Coyote Point?"

"A long time ago." Carrie smiled at the memory. "I'd ride on his shoulders, and we'd have to duck low to get under the branches."

"He used to put me up on his shoulders, too."

Carrie leaned back on her arms with her face to the sun. Her hair fell back and brushed the ground. "At first I didn't understand when he wouldn't take me over here any more. I used to ask him all the time until Mama told me to stop. She said he didn't want to come over here because of Russell." She looked over at me. "Your father. That I had to understand how bad Uncle Emmett felt about Russell being gone. So I stopped asking him."

"He's been over here since Dad disappeared."

"I know, but always alone. I don't think the place has ever been the same for him since then." Carrie sat forward and wrapped her arms around her knees. "I don't guess anything has."

I didn't want to talk about Dad's disappearance or even about how Grandfather had changed. I wanted to go back to that perfect moment with the birds singing but I didn't know how. So instead I stood up and said, "We'd better go back to the house."

"I suppose so." She held out her hand for me to pull her up. "We haven't eaten our quota of Aunt Ruth's brownies yet today."

On the way back through the woods as we talked and laughed and listened for the birds, it was almost like it had been before we had stopped in the clearing. Close enough that I felt the quiet smile inside me that I often felt when the red-eared coyote walked with me.

"Next week you can come over to my house," she said. "We'll watch movies or something."

"What about your father?"

"Mama can get him to say it's okay."

So the next Sunday Grandfather told me how to go up the creek where I'd found the traps and then up the hill and across the field to Carrie's house.

"If you don't dawdle, you can make it in an hour," Grandfather said.

Once in the woods, I dawdled. I was so nervous about facing Carrie's father again and maybe having to talk to him that I didn't think about the red-eared coyote until he barked and stepped out behind me at the Point. I didn't see any way to keep him from following me down the creek, and I really didn't want to. Instead I wondered how mad Carrie would be if I didn't show up at her house.

But then I knew she'd call Grandmother, and Grandmother would think something had happened to me and worry.

I hesitated where the broken-down fence marked the end of Grandfather's property. I hadn't been back over it since the day Joe Kenton had come to the farm, but now I pushed past the fence. At the spot where I'd found the little coyote in the trap, I looked around for signs of a new trap, but there was none.

When I started up the hill that Grandfather said would lead to Carrie's house, I told the coyote to stay behind in hopes he'd do what he did at the edge of the woods and simply stop following me. But here there were still trees.

A little farther up the hill, I stopped and tried again. "Stay here, Red. It's not safe for you to go any closer."

The coyote perked up his ears as if trying to understand, but when I went on, he followed me. I decided that halfway up the hill, I'd turn on him and yell, even throw a stick at him if I had to. I hated the thought of scaring the coyote, but I couldn't lead him into Joe Kenton's backyard.

Suddenly the sound of a gunshot echoed down the creek. Sure that Joe Kenton had spotted my coyote, my heart began beating wildly, but then I realized the shot had been much farther away. My heart slowed its hammering as I let out my breath and turned to the coyote.

He was gone. If I hadn't known the path he liked to use, I'd have never caught sight of him moving lightly along the crest of the hill back toward the Point. He hadn't gone far when the little coyote joined him.

"Good. You'll be safe at the Point," I whispered.

I walked faster now. I was almost to the top when I saw Carrie coming through the trees.

"Hello," she said. "I called Aunt Ruth and she said you were walking over, so I thought I'd come out to meet you."

I was breathing hard from the steep climb. "I hope we're almost there."

She laughed. "It's not much farther and no more hills. I promise."

"Did you hear the gunshot?"

"Daddy's probably shooting pigeons. He doesn't like them to roost in his barns," Carrie said.

"What do they hurt?"

"Their droppings get all over everything. It's a real mess."

"Oh."

When we came out of the trees and could see her house across an open field, she said, "That was a coyote with you, wasn't it?"

I wanted to lie, but I remembered what Grandfather had said. Besides, she'd seen the coyote. "Yes," I said.

As if she'd read my mind, she said, "You don't have to worry. I won't tell Daddy."

We walked along in silence for a minute before Carrie changed the subject. "Mama rented a movie for us to watch."

The movie was just ending when Carrie's father came in with his rifle in the crook of his arm. He carefully placed the gun in a polished wood cabinet with glass doors that held two other guns as well.

I began to think it was time I headed back to the farm even before he turned on me and said, "Carrie tells me you have a way with animals the same as your grandfather does." He sat down across from us in a recliner. "But we already knew that, didn't we? I mean you did let those animals out of my traps. What did you do, kid? Knock them in the head first so they wouldn't bite you?"

"I just opened the traps," I said.

"And the foxes sat there calm-like and let you." His eyes bored into me. "You know they probably died anyway."

"Maybe," I admitted.

Carrie shifted uncomfortably beside me. "How about a soda, Ance?" she said brightly.

"Sounds good," I said, relieved to have an excuse to stop talking to her father.

"Bring us all one, Carrie," her father said.

When she stood, I jumped up, too. "I'll help you."

"She can handle it." Mr. Kenton waved me back down on the couch, and I sat down reluctantly.

"I've been out hunting coyotes," Mr. Kenton said after Carrie went out to the kitchen. "Coyotes are natural sheep killers, you know."

"Grandfather says they eat mice and ground squirrels."

"And lambs and calves and chickens and whatever else the scoundrels can make off with. I tell you, kid, farming is a battle, and if you don't stop them, wild animals will make off with all your profit."

"Grandfather was a farmer."

"He never got rich off it. That's for sure." Joe Kenton laughed. "He used to leave more than half an acre of corn in the field every year for the coons and deer and let a whole field of hay grow up and fall over without cutting it. Now he wants to turn his whole place into some kind of animal preserve. As if he thinks the animals on his place won't come over on me and eat my crops. I tell you I'll shoot the varmits wherever they are before I'll let them put me in the poorhouse."

I glanced over my shoulder to see if Carrie was coming back. There was no sign of her. I looked back in Mr. Kenton's general direction without actually looking at him. "Grandfather doesn't allow hunting on his farm."

Pushing the recliner back, Mr. Kenton settled in it comfortably. "Emmett's always had odd ideas when it comes to animals. His Indian blood showing, I guess. But since Russ ran off, he's gone past just odd to downright strange."

I stared straight at Mr. Kenton's face. "My father's dead." The blood thumped in my ears as I spoke, and I barely noticed Carrie coming toward the couch carrying a tray of drinks.

"There's some that believe that, and some that don't," Mr. Kenton said.

I stood up. "It doesn't matter what you or

anybody else believes. I know the truth. My father died five years ago. He didn't desert us."

"How'd he die, kid? Do you know that?"

I just stared at him without saying anything, and after a strained moment of silence he went on. "Your granddaddy doesn't believe it."

"Daddy!" Carrie set the drinks down on the table.

"I think I'd better go home," I said, glad I had a clear shot at the door.

As I went across the yard, I hoped Carrie wouldn't follow me, but I knew she would.

"Ance, wait," she called, running to catch up with me.

I slowed a little to wait for her.

"Here. You left your jacket." She shoved the coat at me.

"Thanks." I put it on even though I felt too warm. "Look, Carrie, I'm sorry about running out like that."

"I'm the one who's sorry. I don't know what makes Daddy say things like that."

"Because that's what he believes."

"He still shouldn't have said it to you."

We'd both said we were sorry, and there didn't seem to be anything else to say as we walked across the field. When Carrie stopped at the top of the hill that led down to the creek, so did I.

"Daddy wanted to buy Coyote Point from Uncle Emmett last year."

"He'd ruin it," I said.

"He'd make it different, but I don't know that it would be ruined."

"It would be ruined," I repeated.

Carrie's eyes flashed as she said, "Uncle Emmett's way isn't the only way. Daddy isn't always in the wrong."

"He is this time."

"I don't think I want to talk about this any more."

"Good. Neither do I."

"Maybe you just don't want to talk to me at all." Carrie whirled, her hair flying out around her as she ran back toward her house.

I didn't try to stop her.

It was a long walk back to the farm. The sun had been blocked out by clouds, and it began sprinkling even before I got to the cliff. Then in a flashback to winter, the rain began freezing.

As I trudged up the creek with icy bits of rain stinging my face, I kept watching for the coyote. I caught sight of him once up on the hill, but he didn't come any closer.

At the bottom of the cliff, I thought about taking shelter in the cave, but since I was already wet and there was no way I could be any more miserable, I climbed up the cliff path and went on through the woods.

I didn't go inside until I'd done the chores. Fussing all the while, Grandmother made me change out of my wet clothes, wrapped a blanket around me, and fed me hot chocolate. But even after the outside warmed up, I still felt cold inside.

Carrie kept her eyes turned away from me

the next day when I got on the bus. I went past her seat to the back.

On Thursday afternoon I wanted to ask her to come home with me like she always did. I wanted to ask her if there wasn't some way we could be friends again. I even planned out what I might say as I waited for the bell to ring at school, but once I was on the bus, I lost my nerve and passed her seat without saying a word.

She got off at her house, and I got off at the farm. At the barn I rubbed Geraldine so long that Grandmother finally stepped out the back door and hollered for me.

Unable to put if off any longer, I went on to the house to face Grandmother. "Carrie didn't come," I said.

Grandmother smiled. "I know. She's on the phone. She wants to talk to you."

"Carrie?" I said into the receiver and then rushed on before I could lose my nerve again. "Can't we be friends again?"

"You might not want to when you hear what I called to tell you."

"What?"

She hesitated for a second before blurting out, "Oh, Ance, I'm sorry, but Daddy says he shot the coyote today."

I swallowed hard but couldn't say anything.

"He said it got away," Carrie went on. "Maybe it's still alive."

CHAPTER 12

I changed my clothes and was out of the house in five minutes. As I went out the back door Grandmother called after me. "Don't you want to eat something, Ance?"

"I'll get something later."

She followed me outside. "Now, it looks like rain. Don't you stay out there and get wet like you did Sunday."

"Okay, Grandmother. I'll come in if it starts to rain." I'd have promised anything just to get going.

I kept telling myself as I ran across the field and through the trees toward the Point that it might not be my coyotes. There could be other coyotes in the area. And even if it was one of the coyotes I knew, what did I think I was going to do about it? I hadn't even brought the can of wound spray with me.

I started to go back for it, but then with a sinking feeling I knew I'd need more than wound spray if the coyote had been shot.

At the Point, I sat on the rock at the top of the cliff and made myself calm down. I'd come through the woods in such a panic that I hadn't seen so much as a squirrel or a bird. The red-eared coyote would never let me see him.

When a drop of rain hit me, I remembered my promise to Grandmother, but I couldn't go back until I'd found the coyotes.

Walking slower, I went around to the path down the cliff. From far away I heard the soft cooing cry of a mourning dove, and overhead a woodpecker tapped relentlessly into a tree. Across the valley I spotted a deer, but I saw no sign of the coyote.

He'd been more cautious since Sunday, only joining me by the creek and even then keeping a respectable distance. I hadn't seen the little coyote at all.

I was quite a piece down the creek when the coyote bounded down the hill and slid to a stop in front of me.

My heart bounced up light inside me. "Red! You're okay." I'd touched the coyote a few times but only lightly as he passed close to me. He didn't seem to want to be rubbed like a dog. But now I was so relieved to see him, I almost fell on him with a hug.

A low growl in his throat stopped me. Then as I backed off, the growl changed to a whine, and I thought maybe he'd been hurt after all. His ears were laid back almost flat against his head and his tail was between his legs. All of a sudden he flopped down on the ground and rolled over with his feet up in the air.

Gently I brushed through his fur for some sign of a wound, but there was none. When I sat back on my heels, the red-eared coyote sprang back to his feet and took my hand in his mouth.

"It's the little one, isn't it?" I said quietly, my heart no longer so light. "Where is she?"

The coyote led me straight up a hillside that was so steep I had to grab hold of tree saplings to pull myself along. He had to come back for me three times before I made it to the top.

I managed to keep up with him better as I followed him through the trees. Then I lost him again. One minute he'd been in front of my eyes and the next he was gone almost as if the ground had swallowed him.

I tracked him across a muddy creek bed up to a ledge of rocks, but I couldn't see where he'd gone from there. I was searching the creek banks when all at once the coyote stuck his head out from under the rocks. As soon as he saw I was there, his pointed muzzle disappeared again.

I had to get down on my knees in the muddy creek bed before I could even see his hole. A draft of cool air hit my face as I gingerly felt around inside the hole as far as I could reach. This was no burrow the coyotes had dug out.

I stuck my head in the hole, but I couldn't see a thing. I needed a light. "I'll be back," I yelled. The sound echoed back at me.

I didn't expect the coyote to understand, but

when I looked back, he was standing on top of the rocks watching me.

Back at the barn I searched through the jars and cans in the old wooden cupboard. During my first week at the farm, Grandfather had told me to stay out of these shelves. When I'd asked him why, he'd given me a quick rundown of the medicines in the brown jars and warned me that medicines could also be poisons. Now I located the pills that Grandfather had said were good for infections and shoved them and the wound spray in my jacket pocket.

It was getting late, and I ran through my chores, not even taking time to rub Geraldine or pat Jake. Still because of the clouds it was nearly dark before I went in the house to get my flashlight.

"Mercy sakes, child, what happened to you?" Grandmother said when I went through the kitchen.

I looked down at my muddy clothes. "I fell," I said quickly.

"Did you hurt yourself?" She came closer to look for wounds.

"No, I just got muddy. I'm sorry, Grandmother."

"Don't worry about that. I've seen mud before. You should have seen the shape your daddy came in sometimes from over at the Point. I used to tell him that he had to be getting down on his knees and crawling in the mud, and I guess maybe he was." Grandmother smiled and shook her head. "He used to have this thing about finding a cave."

Of course, I thought. The hole the coyote had gone down was a cave. Aloud I asked, "Did he ever find one?"

"No, just lots of holes and more mud." At the word *mud,* Grandmother remembered my clothes again. "Now you get those things off and clean up. Supper's about ready."

"I thought maybe I'd go back over to the Point again," I said. "I've got time before it gets too dark."

"Whatever would you want to go back over there tonight for?" Grandmother asked with a frown.

I said the first thing that came to mind. "I lost my knife when I fell. I want to look for it."

"You couldn't find it in the dark, and it'll still be there tomorrow afternoon."

"If it rains very much, it might sink in the mud."

"Then we'll buy you another knife," Grandfather said from the doorway.

There was no use arguing once Grandfather had said no. As I washed up in the bathroom, I knew I should have told the truth, but now I was ashamed to admit I had lied, and not sure they'd let me go even if I did tell them about the coyote that might be shot and might be down inside the hole that might be a cave.

I stared at the distorted lines of my face in the old mirror and wondered why I'd lied to begin with. Why had I kept the coyote such a secret? Why hadn't I been able to share the red-eared coyote with Grandfather like I did the other animals I saw at the Point?

I moved closer to the mirror until my face looked normal again. Then, although I still stared at the mirror, I didn't see my face anymore. I was seeing the red-eared coyote standing on the ledge of rocks waiting for me to come back.

At supper when Grandfather asked me how things were at the Point, I knew I had my chance to tell him about the coyote, but instead I described the redheaded woodpecker.

Saying I had homework, I escaped to my room early, but then the time ticked by slowly until I finally heard Grandmother and Grandfather getting ready for bed. I put my muddy clothes back on, checking my pockets to make sure I had everything—the spray can, the pills, the flashlight. Then for good measure I stuck some matches and a candle in another pocket.

I waited another hour. Outside the wind was pushing against the house and spattering rain against the windows. The noise helped muffle the sounds I made crawling out the window onto the porch roof. I pulled the window down almost shut and scooted across the roof toward the edge farthest from my grandparents' bedroom.

Easing off the roof feet first, I dropped to the ground. I stood there listening for a moment, but there was no sound except the wind and my own breathing. After checking my pockets one last time, I set off across the field.

Once in the woods, I had to switch on the flashlight to make my way through the trees, and I began to wonder if I'd be able to find the ledge of rock in this thick darkness. My doubts increased when I heard the lonely howl of the coyote coming from the opposite direction than I was headed.

I stopped in the middle of the trees and tried to get my bearings, but everything looked so different at night. Still I was sure I was headed in the right direction.

It wasn't until I sighted the coyote on the rocks with his nose pointed up, howling, that I remembered coyotes could throw their voices. When the coyote turned to look at me, his eyes glittered yellow in the light.

"Poor Red, have you been there waiting for me all this time?" I said. "I hope I don't let you down, but this might not be as easy as opening a trap."

I followed him through the hole. After crawling down a sharp incline, I was able to stand in the room that opened up underground. With a thrill of discovery I flashed my light over the rock walls. Probably no person had ever set foot here before. Then the coyote's whine made me remember why I was here.

The little coyote was huddled under a ledge in the far corner of the room, and even before I crouched down in front of her, I knew she was alive by her fierce growling.

Although my crooning didn't make her stop growling completely, she did let me shine the light over her. The bullet had passed through her leg, shattering the bone in the same leg whose foot had been mangled by the trap. There'd be no hope of her ever using that leg again, and I wondered if she could survive as a cripple even if the wound healed.

Before I could think about the folly of it, I shoved the pills down the coyote's throat. Then I pulled back, surprised that all my fingers were intact. In fact her growling ceased, and I decided she must have thought my grabbing her muzzle was a friendly gesture.

Her growl returned when I sprayed her leg with the medicine, but she was too weak to put up much of a fight.

Leaning back on my heels, I glanced over at the other coyote. "It's up to you now, Red. You'll have to bring her food."

He went over to her and began licking her muzzle, and when she whined he lay down beside her to lend her his warmth.

I'd done all I could do for her. I stood up and flashed my light around the room again. To my left a large opening beckoned me. As I ducked through into the darkness beyond, I wondered if I ought to wait till the next day to explore, but day or night, caves were always dark.

The passageway opened into another room larger than the first. Straw–like rock formations stuck down from the ceiling, and by the time I'd studied all of them, my flashlight was dimming. Still I couldn't resist entering the next passage and exploring just a little farther.

The passage narrowed until I had to crawl, but I was so excited I hardly felt the rocks biting into my hands and knees.

By the time I got to the end of the passageway, my light was so weak it barely penetrated the blackness of whatever lay beyond. I pitched a rock into the void and seconds later heard the splash of water. Since I couldn't see what lay ahead, I reluctantly decided to go back.

The passage was so narrow I couldn't turn but had to back out. I'd been pushing my flashlight along in front of me as I crawled, but now I turned it off and stuck it in my jeans. The dark fell over me like a heavy woolen blanket. I had to fight the urge to take the flashlight back out and made myself keep crawling.

As I crept slowly backward in the dark, I lost all sense of time and distance. I just kept pushing my knees back and inching my hands along feeling for the easiest hold on the rocks under me. When I touched something that wasn't a rock, I switched the flashlight back on.

A rusty pocketknife lay among the rocks. Someone had been here before me.

It had to be Grandfather, I thought as I closed my hand around the knife and smiled. He'd be surprised when I gave him back his knife after so many years.

I left the light on even though I couldn't see where I was going with it, only where I'd been. Finally the passage widened and I inched around frontward again. When I could stand up, I began running because the glow of my flashlight was dimming rapidly. It was going to be a race to get out of the cave before its light gave out completely.

As I ran, the loose rocks shifted and slid under my feet. I grabbed out at the walls, but there was nothing to catch hold of as I fell.

CHAPTER 13

Water running under me woke me. It was so dark I had to feel my eyes to be sure they were open. As I raised up and tried to figure out where I was, my head thumped.

The feel of the cold damp rocks brought it back to me. I had been running to get out of the cave and had fallen.

A big knot was rising on the back of my head, but I was more worried about my flashlight. Remembering the candle and matches I'd put in my pocket, I breathed with relief. Then my heart sank again as I pulled out the matchbook. My pocket was soaked; the matches ruined.

Pushing down panic, I began feeling around for the flashlight. The passage wasn't that wide. It had to be there somewhere. When my hand fell on it, I whooped with happiness, but my joy was short-lived. Nothing happened when I pushed the switch. The batteries were dead.

As I sat there, my useless flashlight in one hand and my wet matches in the other, the dark around me changed, grew thicker, and became something besides simply air with no light.

I shoved the things back in my pockets and began moving along the passageway. Even without light I could feel my way along it to the larger open room, but when the passage began narrowing, I realized I was going in the wrong direction. I retraced my steps, stopping when I could no longer touch both sides of the passage.

I scooted my feet along for a few more steps, but I was afraid I might go off in the wrong direction without the walls to guide me.

I'd have to wait till morning and hope some shaft of light would penetrate the darkness of the cave to guide me back to the opening.

As I sat there listening to water dripping in the cave, the silence became as oppressive as the darkness. I couldn't tell how much time passed. I tried counting to sixty several times, but when I stopped counting I had no more idea of the space of time it took a minute to pass than I had before.

After a long time, I tried the light again. No glow came from it. Then as time crept by, I wondered how long it would take to die inside here.

Frowning, I shook myself. I wasn't going to die. All I had to do was wait till morning. Then there would be light from somewhere, or my matches would dry out.

When I reached in my pocket to pull them out into the air, I touched the knife that had to be Grandfather's. For a minute my hand closed around it, and I felt better. He'd remember this cave. He'd find me.

Somehow I dozed then, but when I awoke, the darkness was still complete. With shaky hands I carefully tore one of the paper matches loose and pulled it across the striking mark. I could feel the end of the match crumbling without a spark. I tried three before I gave up.

Sure that it had to be morning by now, I searched the dark around me for a hint of light. It was a long time before I admitted to myself that there wasn't going to be any shaft of light to follow out of the cave.

Then I thought of Grandmother finding my bed empty. I wondered what she and Grandfather would do, and my hand closed around the knife in my pocket again. The feel of it gave me courage to keep staring into the black dark.

I knew I should have told Grandfather about the coyote. He would have understood. He might have even been able to tell me how to better help the little coyote. I wondered how she was doing and if the red-eared coyote was still keeping watch by her or if he'd gone out to hunt for their breakfast. Or maybe lunch. I had no idea what time it was.

I wished the red-eared coyote would come back in the cave to keep me company. Maybe if I howled, he would. It had sometimes worked when I'd walked down the creek. I'd howl, and he'd come out of the bushes ahead of me and bark a little as though laughing at my efforts to imitate him.

The howl echoed strangely in the cave, but it made me feel better. I threw back my head and howled even louder.

I didn't know the coyote was there until he barked right beside me. I jumped, and I heard the coyote's toenails on the rock as he scrambled away from me.

"Sorry, Red." I wasn't sure whether he was still there or not until he sniffed my hand. "I'll bet you can get out of here," I said.

He took my hand in his mouth and gave it a little pull. When he turned loose, I stood up with my hand lightly touching his fur. Maybe if I could keep up with him he'd lead me out of here.

Whenever the coyote moved away from my hand, he always came back.

"How can you see your way?" I asked, gratefully touching him again after stumbling and falling. Then I realized he didn't have to see. He was smelling his way out of the cave.

When I finally saw light up ahead, the coyote, his duty to me done, trotted back to his mate. As much as I wanted to push out of the hole into the daylight, I followed him and looked at the little coyote's leg. She growled a little but hardly moved when I sprayed the wound again.

I didn't waste another second as I exploded out of the hole and fell face down in the muddy water that had gathered in the creek during the night. Nothing had ever looked or felt as good as that mud.

It was still raining, but I didn't care. I held my face up to the raindrops as I walked through the trees, touching their branches and trying to keep from laughing out loud.

Maybe I did laugh out loud and that's how Grandfather found me. Water dripped off his coat, and his face was so gray and drawn with weariness that my laugh died in my throat.

"Grandfather, you shouldn't be out in this rain."

"I've been searching for you, boy."

"I'm sorry." I dropped my eyes to the ground and then jerked them back up to his. "You haven't been searching long, have you?"

"I had to wait till Carrie Ruth came to stay with Ruth. They wanted to call the police, but I made them promise to wait till I came back." Grandfather let out a long breath. "They probably think we're both lost by now."

"I'm sorry," I said again.

"It was just like the other time," Grandfather said. "It was raining that time, too, though this is a shower compared to the rain we had that day."

"You mean when Dad disappeared?" I felt worse than ever.

"Where have you been, boy?"

I told him about the coyote then and the cave and how I'd hit my head. He reached around and gently touched the knot on the back of my head. I kept talking. "I thought you'd find me, that maybe you'd remember the cave."

"I don't know about any caves."

"But I found your knife." I held the knife out toward him.

His hands trembled as he took the knife from me. As he stared at it, he seemed to forget the rain falling on him.

He was silent so long, I finally said, "Hadn't we better go home so Grandmother won't worry?"

Grandfather looked away through the trees, and I barely recognized his voice when he said, "Show me this cave."

When I started to argue, he looked at me, and I felt almost like I was back in the silent blackness of the cave even though the rain still hit my face.

I didn't say anything more until we got to the ledge of rocks. "There's a hole that goes under those rocks."

When he clambered down on his knees in the muddy water, I grabbed his arm. "You can't go in there, Grandfather." He pulled away from me, and I searched for a way to stop him. "We don't have a light."

Without a word, he pulled a flashlight out of his pocket and went down on his belly to crawl through the hole. Swallowing a great gulp of the free outside air, I followed him.

Grandfather was already standing up looking around the cave when I scrambled back to my feet. "Will you look at the coyote?" I asked.

"Not now, boy. Where'd you find this?" He held out the knife again.

"It's a long way, Grandfather, and hard walking."

His face softened for just a minute. "You were in there a long time, weren't you, boy?"

"I'd still be there if it hadn't been for the coyote." I nodded toward the red-eared coyote who was standing guard over his mate.

"I don't blame you for being afraid."

I started to deny it, but then I just said, "It was so dark, Grandfather."

"You don't have to go with me. Just show me which direction."

I couldn't let him go alone. He was breathing hard already and coughing. So I led the way, thankful for the bright light his flashlight put out. We sloshed through water running along the passages. "There wasn't this much water a while ago," I said.

"It's the rain," Grandfather said. "Caves can fill fast when it's raining hard."

When we got to the passage where I found the knife, I explained how the passageway narrowed.

"Then I guess we'd better go in backward," Grandfather said. He was coughing more and his breath was short.

"I think we should go home."

"Don't you know whose knife this is, boy?" Grandfather grabbed my shoulder in a tight grip and pushed the knife close to my face. "I can't go back till I find him."

I shivered as a chill ran through me, and Grandfather relaxed his hold. "But maybe it'd be better if you waited here," he said.

"In the dark?"

He fished under his coat deep in his pocket and pulled out a book of matches.

After I lit my candle, I watched him back away into the passage. I stared at the shadows the candle flame threw on the rock walls and followed Grandfather's progress through the tunnel of rock by his coughs and the rocks shifting under him. Then there was a splash, and I knew I couldn't just sit there.

I couldn't make myself back into the passage. So I went headfirst, holding my lighted candle ahead of me, but when I had to start crawling, it went out. Still I kept going.

At the end of the tunnel, I saw no light. "Grandfather," I yelled, my heart thumping heavily. "Where are you, Grandfather?"

The sound echoed back over and over. When the last echo died away I could barely keep from shouting again, but then I heard Grandfather cough.

"I'm okay, Little Russ. I'm okay."

They were the words I wanted to hear, but his voice was so strange that I wasn't sure I could believe them. "Did you lose your light?" I asked. "Do you want me to light the candle?"

"No," he said, "I need the dark for a minute."

I sat there staring out at the blackness while my heart kept beating wildly. I had to try twice before I was able to form the words. "Did you find him?"

"I did."

Suddenly Grandfather flicked on his light and let it play a minute on a wide stream of water running down the walls into a large pool below.

Then he waded around the edge of the pool till he was below me. "Give me a hand up, boy."

After I pulled him up, I crawled out backward while he crawled forward, scooting the light in front of him and stopping often to cough. We were so close I couldn't keep from seeing the tears that wet his cheeks.

Once we were in the room where we could stand upright again, I looked back toward the passage and asked, "What happened?"

"The rain. Russ must have found a way down into here that day. You know the sun was shining bright that morning when he left, and the weatherman we listened to didn't forecast any rain. Russ probably never knew it was raining until it was too late."

"What do you mean?"

"That day it rained like you never saw before. The water must have poured into the cave flooding the passage." Grandfather stopped talking and switched off his light. After a minute, he said, "Your mother was right all along, Little Russ. He drowned." His voice broke as he went on. "I should never have doubted him."

Not knowing what else to do, I reached for Grandfather in the dark and hugged him. He stiffened but then his arms went around me, too.

After a minute Grandfather pulled away, flicked on the light, and said, "We'd better get on home, boy."

When we got back to the room with the entrance, water was spilling through the hole in a steady stream. The red-eared coyote was outside barking back through the hole. The little coyote was up on her three good legs under the opening.

"She can't get out," Grandfather said when he saw her. "We'll have to help her."

"She doesn't like people," I warned.

"Can't see as I blame her." He stopped in front of her and clucked his tongue a few times. "Easy, girl. We're just going to set you outside."

He looked around at me. "You go on out, boy, and I'll hand her up to you."

The water half filled the hole, but I pushed through it out into the creek. When Grandfather lifted the coyote up, I took hold of her and pulled her out. She growled, and I quickly let her go. She scrambled away from me to where the red-eared coyote waited.

Then I helped pull Grandfather out of the hole into the muddy creek. After we climbed out of the water, we rested a minute on the bank, paying no attention to the rain. We were already soaked.

"What's Grandmother going to say?"

"She'll have the doc out to poke and prod on me and make me take more of that nasty cough syrup." Grandfather looked over at me. "She might even make you take a few doses."

"But what about Dad?"

"I don't know." Grandfather got up. "She wanted to believe that Russ would come back one day just like he'd never been away and we'd all start over again. This will be a grief to her."

"Maybe it will just be a different way of starting over."

"Maybe so, Little Russ. Maybe so." He put his hand on my arm. "Now you go on and find our way back to the house. All this rain is messing up my sense of direction."

As we started away from the creek, the coyote howled behind us. The sound filled me with a strange sadness, and I looked back at him for a minute. "He's telling me goodbye, isn't he, Grandfather?"

"Could be. The little one's about to find pups, and he'll be busy taking care of his family."

The coyote howled one last time before he trotted down off the ledge of rocks and followed the little coyote into the trees. In seconds they'd vanished from sight. "Do you think I'll ever see him again?"

"Hard to say."

As we walked through the trees, Grandfather's coughing was all that broke the silence between us, but there in the woods, we didn't need words.

Then as I caught the first glimpse of the farmhouse through the trees, I asked, "Do you think Grandmother is watching at the window?"

"I wouldn't doubt it."

I ran into the clear, jumped up and down, and waved. A second later Carrie came out on the porch with something in her arms.

When Grandfather caught up with me I

asked, "What's she got?" I had to make myself slow down to keep pace with Grandfather.

"Foolish girl," Grandfather said. "She brought you the ugliest pup anybody's ever likely to see."

"A pup?" I looked up at Grandfather. "But I thought you said you and Grandmother were too old to fool with a pup."

"I guess we're not that old," Grandfather said, his voice sounding cross.

I knew he wasn't really cross, and I couldn't help myself. I gave him another hug.

He pushed me gently away. "Go on, Little Russ. I know you're wanting to run. I'll be along."

As I ran across the field to meet Carrie, she ran to meet me, too, her hair flying out behind her. She shoved the ugly little pup at me with a giggle that became a laugh when the pup began licking my face.

Then we both waited in the rain to walk the rest of the way across the field with Grandfather.